MURDER IN A SAFE HAVEN

An Irish murder mystery with a wicked twist

DAVID PEARSON

THE BOOK FOLKS

Paperback edition published by

The Book Folks

London, 2020

ISBN 978-1-913516-89-5

www.thebookfolks.com

Marjorie, for providing endless support and encouragement over many years.

Chapter One

It was later than usual in the year when Detective Superintendent Mick Hays got his boat back in the water. The weather had been foul, with winter holding its grip on the west of Ireland right into May. Heavy grey clouds had hung over the county persistently through the normally bright month of April, and rainfall had been almost double the average for the time of year.

But in the last week, summer had arrived in earnest, and Hays wasted no time in getting his beloved yacht ready for use. His life partner, Senior DI Maureen Lyons, had spent many long hours with Hays scraping the hull, and repainting it with copper-coloured anti-foul paint, while Hays replaced the sacrificial anodes placed here and there along the underside and on the rudder. Lyons had also cleaned the interior of the vessel comprehensively, polishing the dark oak and brass fittings, and laundering the seat covers, so that by the time the sloop went back to its natural habitat, it was looking resplendent.

Lyons didn't enjoy sailing. She was inclined to sea sickness, which made excursions out across Galway Bay a misery for both of them. So, Hays had rigged the sloop by bringing all the controls back into the cockpit, allowing him to sail single-handedly when the weather was fair. In stiffer winds he brought crew with him – usually one or two – to man the foredeck and help generally navigate against the weather and the tide.

On this occasion, he set off from the sailing club at Oranmore with the main sail set, and the massive Genoa foresail scooping as much of the light wind as possible to bring *Natalie* up to almost four knots. *Natalie* wouldn't have been his first choice, but it was considered bad luck to change the name of a yacht, so he left it alone. The boat had been bought for him by Lyons when she had been awarded a bonus by the Gardaí following a particularly heroic capture of a murderous villain a few years ago.

For the first excursion of the season, Hays decided on a very gentle outing to refamiliarize himself with all the controls, and test the equipment that had lain dormant over the winter, such as the compasses, the GPS, the radio and depth finder. Hays' plan was to hug the coast out as far as Rinville West, and then carry on till he was at Twain Island. Then, depending on the sea state, he would bring the boat about and sail across to Galway harbour, tie the boat up, and meet Maureen for lunch at one of the seafood restaurants on the quays.

Things were going well out at sea. The boat was responding as expected, and all the gear seemed to be working as it should. Hays was getting his sea legs, and had just tacked across to bring *Natalie* onto a broad reach and steer a course for the entrance to Galway harbour when he felt a thud against the hull up front. Hays secured the helm with the two ropes that would keep the boat on course, and climbed out of the cockpit, walking carefully up along the windward deck to the forepeak. He looked about, and soon spotted the dark shape of what could have been an animal, or a floating sack of some rubbish carelessly discarded by someone onshore.

Something spurred Hays to investigate further. He got back to the stern of the vessel and let out the sails so that they were flapping in the breeze. He started the engine, and turned the boat through 180 degrees, and in a couple of minutes he was alongside the dark shape. Using his boathook, he caught the black hulk by one edge and turned it over. The partly decomposed face of a man appeared.

Hays wasted no time in using his radio on channel sixteen to issue a Pan-Pan call-back to the coastguard station. He explained what he had found, and requested assistance.

"I can't get the body back on board – it's waterlogged. Can you get the lifeboat out – they'll be able to manhandle it onto their boat. I'll stay on station until they arrive," Hays said.

"I'll need your GPS co-ordinates, sir," the coastguard operator said.

"Oh, yes, sure. Hang on a minute."

Hays went below and took note of the grid reference displayed on the GPS system that was screwed to the bulkhead at the navigation station. He then read them out to the coastguard.

There was nothing to do now but wait. It would take Galway's D-lass lifeboat ten minutes to turn out, and then a further ten to fifteen minutes to reach Hays' position across the bay. He took out his mobile phone, and fortunately was close enough to land to get a signal. He called Maureen Lyons.

"Hi, Mick. How's it going? Boat all OK?"

"Hi. Boat's fine. But listen, I've come across a body in the water. The lifeboat is on its way to recover it now."

"That would be a dead body, I presume, Mick? God, it would take you wouldn't it, and on a Sunday as well! What do you need me to do?" Lyons said.

"Well best get Dr Dodd out for starters. Have him meet you by the lifeboat station in the city so he can give us a view on the body before it gets too mucked up."

"Yeah, OK."

"It'll take me a good while to get back there, so I'll need you to take charge at the quayside. I'll meet you at the mortuary as soon as I can. Is that OK?" Hays said.

"Oh, sure. I was just hanging around waiting for a dead body to turn up on my only day off anyway. But yes, that's fine. Are you OK?" Lyons said.

"Yes, I'm good. I'll see you soon."

* * *

Hays could see the lifeboat approaching, throwing up a large white spray from its twin Mercury engines. He knew the coxswain of the Galway lifeboat from sailing, and he knew Peadar Bolger would be careful how he approached. On cue, Hays' radio sprang to life.

"Galway Lifeboat to yacht *Natalie*. How do you read?"

"Hi, Peadar. It's Mick Hays here. I read you clearly," Hays said.

"Roger, Mick, switch to working channel 44, over."

Hays adjusted the radio and clicked the transmit button.

"I have the body secured on the leeward side now, so if you can approach slowly on my starboard you'll be able to get it, over."

"Roger, Mick. Stand by."

The lifeboat slowed to a crawl and approached carefully, rocking gently in the swell. Two men appeared on the port side of the RIB and clipped themselves onto the safety tape running along inside the boat. They reached over the side, and although it was a struggle, they slowly manhandled the dark, sodden form back into their bright orange boat.

Bolger waved to Hays as the lifeboat took off again and headed back to the city. As they sped away, Hays used the radio again.

"Peadar, can you hook up with DI Lyons when you get in. She'll be at the quayside with our pathologist Dr Julian Dodd, over."

"Sure, Mick, will do. Over and out."

Chapter Two

Lyons arrived at the pier at the same time as Dr Julian Dodd. She sat into his shiny black Lexus as they were waiting for the lifeboat to complete the journey back into the harbour.

"Morning, Doctor. How's tricks?"

Dr Dodd was a small man, but what he lacked in stature he made up for in personality. He was always immaculately dressed, and today was no exception. He wore expensive fawn, cavalry twill trousers; what looked like a cashmere pullover on top of a twill check shirt, and stout brown leather brogues with punched toecaps that were highly polished.

"I hope you haven't got me out here on a wild goose chase, Inspector. I'm due at my daughter's place in half an hour for Sunday lunch. Remember the dead sheep out at Roundstone?" Dodd said, referring to a time when Garda Pascal Brosnan had called out the cavalry when what he thought was a body was discovered washed up on the rocks at Dog's Bay. The 'body' turned out to be a dead sheep that had fallen into the sea and drowned.

"I think Superintendent Hays knows the difference between a sheep and a body, Doctor," Lyons said defensively.

"Let's hope so, Maureen, let's hope so."

The lifeboat arrived in the harbour with its gruesome cargo. Fortunately, the tide was high, which made the job of bringing the body ashore a little bit easier. After a few minutes, the corpse was lying on its back on top of a plastic body-bag on the harbour wall.

Dr Dodd greeted the lifeboat cox whom he knew from various other encounters over the years.

"Morning, Peadar. What have you brought me today?"

"Hi, Doc. Looks like a male, possibly in his late thirties, but he could be younger."

"Hmm. Anything else floating around near him out there?" Dodd said.

"No, but I doubt if that's where he went in. The tide would have carried him out there, and he's been in quite a while – long enough for the body's gasses to bring him back to the surface anyway," Bolger said.

Lyons turned, and walked a few paces away from the scene. The smell of the body was not pleasant, and it was not that long since she had breakfast.

"So, he's been in there at least four days," Dodd said.

"Yes, but not much longer. There would be very little of him left if he'd been in there more than five days. He's not in bad shape, except of course that he's dead," Bolger said.

Dodd bent down over the body and examined the exposed head without disturbing it.

"Look at this thing at the back of his head – I don't think it's a bullet wound – that would have blown much of his face away. But he's had a pretty nasty whack on the head, and it's not from the rocks. Better get him back to the lab till we see what's what. Thanks, Peadar, and thank the lads for me too."

"Right you are, Doc. We'll leave him to you then."

Lyons returned to where the doctor was getting back up a little stiffly. A black Mercedes van without markings had arrived, and two men dressed in plastic coveralls were standing by to load the body into the vehicle and take it back to Dr Dodd's lab in the grounds of Galway University Hospital.

"Any initial thoughts, Doc?" Lyons asked.

"I'll know more later, but right now I'm going to lunch with my family, Inspector. I'll see to our friend here after that."

* * *

Lyons followed the black van back to the grounds of the hospital. The Mercedes pulled up at the entrance to the mortuary which was positioned in an annexe at the back of the main building. There was no sign of Hays' car, so Lyons went into the hospital and got herself a coffee from the little shop in the reception area. She took her drink back outside and sat on a low wall, enjoying the heat of the sun taking the chill of the morning's events away.

Twenty minutes later, Mick Hays' silver Mercedes rolled into the car park and stopped beside Lyons.

"Hi. What's the story?" he said, getting out and blipping the key fob to lock his car.

Lyons updated Hays on what they knew so far, and told him about the wound to the back of the victim's head.

"I see. So, we could have a murder on our hands. Great!" Hays said.

"I guess," Lyons replied. "But I don't want to get everyone all excited till we know what's going on. No need to disturb their weekend till we have a confirmation, and a couple of hours won't make any difference to the victim, that's for sure."

"OK. It's your call. Why don't we go and get some lunch then, and after that I'll make a statement for you about finding the body."

"Sounds like a plan. Where do you fancy?" Lyons said.

Hays looked at his watch.

"We're just in time to catch service at the Meerick, if you fancy it?"

"Yes, that would be lovely. But we'll need to get a uniform out to stand guard over the body until the PM. Can you set that up while I call the hotel?" Lyons said.

"Sure."

A few minutes later a squad car arrived at the mortuary, and a uniformed Garda received his gruesome assignment from Hays.

"I'll have to come back to identify the body to Dodd when the PM is starting, so give me a call, won't you," Hays said to the man, and then both he and Lyons set off in their respective cars for the city centre.

When they were seated at the table in the luxurious surroundings of the Hotel Meerick's top floor dining room, and had ordered lunch, Lyons asked Hays, "How's the lovely *Natalie* then?" as if she was another woman in Hays' life.

"She's terrific. It was great to get out again after such a long winter. Everything is in fine order. The masthead lamp seems to be out, but that's about it. I'll get Gerry the boatman down at the club to sort it."

"Let's hope we get some decent weather for a while now so you can get to use her a bit more. Any plans for any longer journeys?" Lyons asked.

"Ah, you know. There's talk of a trip down to Crosshaven for the regatta in July, but it's probably all talk. Would you fancy it?"

"Sure, as long as I can go by road! I'd join you there for the craic, but don't ask me to sail around County Kerry in the Atlantic swell – no chance."

"Land lubber!" Hays said with a big smile.

Chapter Three

It was mid-afternoon when Hays and Lyons got the call to return to the mortuary having had a delightful, leisurely lunch at the city centre hotel. They buzzed the door at the entrance, and one of Dodd's assistants released the lock to let them in. Dodd was dressed in a heavy green rubber apron, blue vinyl gloves and a blue cloth cap over his mop of grey hair.

"Ah, detectives, I'm just about to get started, do come in and join us. Can you confirm, Superintendent, that this is the man you found in the sea earlier today?" Dodd said.

"Yes – that's the one, Doc. No doubt."

Dodd was accompanied by two lab assistants, one male and one female, who followed behind him like adoring puppies and hung on his every word.

The doctor walked around the bright stainless-steel gurney where the victim was lying on his back with a support under his head, as if he were stalking the man. But both Hays and Lyons knew that he was observing at every new step, sizing up his quarry from every angle.

With a nod from the good doctor, the assistants moved in and started to remove the man's clothes. They started with his jacket, and then took off his shirt, finishing with his trousers and socks, but leaving his underpants in place in order to preserve a modicum of dignity.

The victim was in reasonably good condition. His skin was a kind of blue-grey colour, but he was not overweight, and there were signs that he was no stranger to exercise. Lyons guessed that he was probably in his late twenties or early thirties.

As Hays continued to observe the doctor at his work, Lyons donned her own blue gloves, took the man's jacket from the female assistant, and went through the pockets. She did the same with his trousers, but found nothing other than a cotton handkerchief, some loose change, and a plastic tortoiseshell comb with a few teeth missing that had miraculously remained in an inside pocket. She noted that his jacket was an expensive make. There was no wallet or any other form of identification in any of his clothing, but in one of his pockets was a clump of receipts, some of which were just about identifiable as being from shops in Galway. That told the detectives the deceased was most likely a local man.

Lyons returned to the table where Dodd was continuing his exploration of the man's head. His other assistant had shaved the hair away from the wound, giving the doctor a better view, and Dodd was gently probing the area with some ghastly implement or other.

"Hmm. This is interesting. I'd say this was inflicted with some sort of metal bar, circular in shape, and possibly with a point at the end. It's gone a long way in, so some considerable force was used."

"Is that what killed him?" Hays said.

"I should imagine so, Inspector, wouldn't you?" Dodd said.

"You're the pathologist, Doctor. I'll go by whatever you say."

"Very gracious, I'm sure. But there is something more here."

Dodd took up a hand-held magnifying glass and peered into the wound. He signalled to his female assistant to approach, and she drew close with a kidney-shaped metal dish and a few instruments.

Dodd took tweezers from the girl and delicately removed a small fragment.

"Ferrous oxide, if I'm not mistaken," he said triumphantly, dropping the tiny specimen in the dish.

"Do you mean rusty iron, Doctor?" Lyons said.

"Precisely, Inspector. We can have it analysed, but I'd wager it's from some sort of industrial place – maybe a building site, or a metal fabrication outfit – but that's not for me to speculate."

"It's a start, Doc. Anything else?"

"Give me time, dear girl, all will be revealed. If you want to get on, I'll have a full report on your desk in the morning."

Hays, who had been standing observing the proceedings without saying anything, spoke up, "Yeah, let's get out of here, Maureen, the smell of formaldehyde is making me ill!"

* * *

It was just after eight in the morning when they reached the Garda station the following morning. They had phoned around the previous evening asking everyone to be in early, outlining what they knew so far, which, they had to admit, wasn't much. Hays went off upstairs to see to his many administrative duties as Detective Superintendent, leaving Maureen Lyons to assume the role of Senior Investigating Officer.

Eamon Flynn and Sally Fahy were waiting for Hays and Lyons to arrive, and started setting up the preliminaries.

Lyons opened the proceedings.

"Right, everyone, the first thing we need to do is to establish the identity of our John Doe," she said, pointing with her pen at the photo that had been pinned to the whiteboard.

"Sally, will you get John to start trawling the missing persons. The usual – start with Galway City and then move out incrementally till the whole area is covered."

"Surely anyone that's gone missing would be in PULSE?" Fahy said.

"Not necessarily, Sally. Anyway, I haven't seen any memos about any misper that fits the description, have you? The smaller stations don't always update the system, so do a ring around, and let me know if you get a hit," Lyons said.

"Righto, boss."

"Eamon, will you check in with Dodd as soon as the hour gets decent. We left him yesterday just as he was wielding his scalpel in a menacing fashion. Sometimes I think that man enjoys his work far too much!"

"OK. What are you going to do, boss?" Flynn asked, in his usual rather direct manner.

"I, dear man, am going to do some navigation, am I not?"

"I see," Flynn said, not seeing at all.

"Let's reassemble at twelve o'clock – see what we've all managed to find."

Lyons went to her office and cleared a large space on the desk which was, as usual, cluttered with all sorts of paperwork – most of it irrelevant to her work as a detective. She logged onto her PC and located a marine map for Galway Bay. She rescaled it to cover the area that she wanted, and then sent it to the station's large A3 inkjet printer. Five minutes later she had the map spread out on the desk and was studying it carefully. Lyons paid special attention to the small arrows that indicated tidal flows and currents on the map. She tapped her pen on her lips as she tried to figure out exactly what the chart was telling her. She called Mick Hays on the internal phone.

"Mick, have you got a couple of minutes? I can pop up if you have."

"Give me half an hour – I'm just finishing something here. Then come on up."

"Gotcha! And make sure you have the coffee on," she said, and hung up before he could complain.

She was still studying the chart when her own phone rang.

"Lyons," she said.

"Ah, good morning, Inspector. It's Dr Dodd. Look, I'll be sending across my report later this morning when we get his bloods back from the toxicology lab, but I thought you might like to know that we found something a bit odd after you left yesterday," he said in a way that Lyons thought could have been somewhat accusatory.

"And what was that, Doctor?"

"Chummy here had sand between his toes, and in his socks. I'm getting it analysed as we speak. It might give you a clue as to where he went in or how he came to be there. Off the record, and based on a preliminary look at the residue under the microscope, I'd say the sand was largely very fine shell particles. That kind of sand is peculiar to certain specific locations around the bay, but I'll know more later."

"I see. Anything else?"

"Yes, as you ask. Stomach contents indicate that he had eaten around two or three hours before he died, although to be truthful, the food was very putrefied. Burger and chips, if I'm not mistaken."

"OK, thanks, Doc. Anything more on the weapon?" Lyons said.

"Give us a chance, Inspector. The labs aren't even open yet!"

"Sorry, no worries. Talk later."

Chapter Four

Lyons explained the message she had received from Dr Julian Dodd when she was in Hays' spacious office with the chart she had printed earlier spread out on his desk.

"He said that from an initial examination, he thought the sand found in the victim's shoes was actually composed of small grains of seashells. What does that tell us?" Lyons said.

"Let's have a look," Hays said, peering closely at the colourful sheet before him.

"Well, the sand on the seabed all along the north coast of the Bay is largely formed by rocks that have been ground down over the years by the motion of the sea, but when you get to Golam Head, the composition of the sand changes. From there all the way around to Carna, the sand is mostly ground up seashells, like it is out at Dog's Bay – see, it's marked on the chart here," Hays said pointing to the area around Lettermullan.

"But surely, if he went in up there somewhere, he'd never have ended up where you found him?" Lyons said.

"Let's have a look at the tidal chart, see what it tells us."

Hays went to his PC and brought up a series of maps and charts of the area from a number of sources. While they meant nothing to Lyons, as a seafaring man, Hays was better able to interpret the various models.

"Yes, see here," he said, tracing the blunt end of his pen across the screen, "the prevailing current along the northern coast of the Bay is west to east. The current then swirls in around the inner Bay and harbour, and goes back out largely along the southern shore. There are a few variations, but that's the norm. And if the wind was from the prevailing south-west direction, then the body could easily have been brought in to where I found it from Golam Head," Hays said.

"Are you sure though? It's a bit of a stretch, isn't it?" Lyons said.

"I don't think so. If he was chucked in out there on a falling tide, he would have been carried out into the current. Worth following up anyway. Have we any word on who he is yet?"

"No, not yet. So, do you think I should go out there and see if anyone saw anything?" Lyons said, still unsure of the quality of the information she had been given.

"That's up to you. But try not to tread on the locals' toes too much – we don't need some irate inspector from out that way giving us grief."

"What station looks after Golam, or whatever you call it?" Lyons said.

"It's kind of on the border between Carraroe and Roundstone. I'd give Carraroe a call first – see if they are interested, and if not, look up your old friend Pascal Brosnan."

"OK, thanks for your help. I'd never have figured all that out on my own. I'll catch you later."

* * *

When Lyons got back downstairs, she called Carraroe Garda Station. The sergeant advised her that they were very busy and couldn't allocate anyone to her case for a few days at least. Apparently, they were hot on the trail of a gang stealing high-value farm machinery, and every available officer was deployed to that task.

Lyons then called Roundstone station. The phone was answered by Mary Fallon. Mary was a young Garda recently qualified from the training college at Templemore. She had been originally allocated to Sergeant Séan Mulholland in Clifden, but Mulholland – not being used to having female members of the force under his command – had re-assigned her to Roundstone where Pascal Brosnan and herself manned the small Garda station at the edge of the village.

"Hi, Mary. It's Maureen here from Galway. Superintendent Hays fished a dead body out of the water yesterday, and we think there's a possibility the deceased may have gone in somewhere out near Golam Head. I've been onto Carraroe and they have no one available. Do you think either you or Pascal could meet me at Kilnatrá in about 45 minutes to see if we can find out anything?"

Kilnatrá was a remote spot on the coast of Galway Bay. It got its name, which means church by the beach, from a time when Roman Catholic worship was suppressed in Ireland. Priests would gather a congregation from around the locality and say Mass on the beach. In some places, small buildings were erected to facilitate the ceremonies in poor weather, but if there ever had been one at Kilnatrá, it was by now long gone.

"Oh, blimey. Yes, of course, Inspector. Do you need both of us?" Fallon said.

"No, I don't think so. I'll have someone with me anyway, so just one of you will do. Is that OK?"

"Yes, sure. I'll have a chat with Pascal and one of us will be there. Thanks."

Lyons then went to the open plan where Sally Fahy was working away at her PC. There was no sign of Eamon Flynn.

"Hi, Sally," Lyons said, "where's Eamon?"

"He's out following up on the mispers to see if he can get anything. I think he's gone down to the docks with a picture of yer man to ask around."

"Oh, right. Well can you come with me? We have to meet someone from the Roundstone station out at Kilnatrá. Mick thinks our man may have gone into the water there," Lyons said.

"Crikey! That's a bit of a long way off, isn't it?"

"Yes, it is, but Mick had a good look at the charts and the tides and stuff. The sand that was inside chummy's socks is composed largely of finely ground seashells, and that's the nearest place with that particular kind of sand. And the tides work too, so he's asked us to look into it."

Sally Fahy knew better than to challenge the instincts of the superintendent, especially not with Lyons, so she was happy to go along with the excursion. Anyway, it would get her out of the office for a few hours.

* * *

"Sounds like a hell of a long shot to me, Mary," Pascal Brosnan said when Mary Fallon told him about the call she had taken from Lyons.

"Will you go?" he asked.

"Yeah, sure. I'll give you a shout if anything develops."

"I won't be holding my breath," Brosnan said, finishing his mug of morning tea.

Mary Fallon took the station's brightly coloured Hyundai squad car, and drove out along the R341 through the village of Roundstone, which was still largely asleep at this hour of the day, and on towards Recess. The weather was holding up nicely, and the sky was sprinkled with fluffy cotton wool clouds that occasionally obscured the bright sun. The lakes that punctuated the bog liberally on either side of the road were swollen with all the recent rain, and the sun danced on their surfaces giving them a shimmering, silvery look.

Just before the Anglers' Return, Mary turned right onto the R342 towards the Zetland Country House Hotel, and then right again onto the R340 that would take her in a wide loop eventually leading to Kilnatrá.

Kilnatrá was more a township than a village. It made the junction between the two arms of the R340, and right at the confluence of the two roads, the only building of significance stood. It was a hostelry called Tigh Oisrí, which, translated from the Irish language, meant the Oyster House. It took its name from the bay which stretched out in front of it, which in turn was named after the rich oyster beds along the shoreline.

Mary arrived first, and parked the Garda car in the car park at the front of the pub. She was immediately taken by the amazing view out over Galway Bay. Far offshore a wooden fishing boat was bobbing about in the gentle swell, presumably trying for mackerel, although it was in all honesty too early in the season for that species yet, but they would be plentiful in another month.

Lyons and Fahy arrived a few minutes later, and when they were all out of their vehicles, they greeted each other warmly.

Lyons gave Mary a quick outline of the situation and then suggested that they all go into the pub and try and rustle up a cup of coffee.

* * *

Inside the building, there was rather surprisingly a hive of industry. A man in his fifties, overweight, dressed in a rather scruffy grey T-shirt and sweating profusely, was dashing around with sets of cutlery wrapped in colourful paper napkins that he placed three at a time on the small round tables. Behind the bar, an equally plump woman with short grey hair, dressed in a floral pinafore, was laying out plates of dark brown bread.

Lyons caught the man's attention and asked if they could get three coffees.

The man was not best pleased, but recognising them as members of the Gardaí, reluctantly agreed.

"It will be a few minutes, ladies. Delia is very busy. We're expecting a bus tour in about an hour, and they'll be looking for their lunch."

"Oh, sorry. There's no rush. Whenever," Lyons said, smiling.

"Do you get many tours?" she said.

"That we do. Two or three times a week from now on, and they can be a fussy lot," the man said, glad to have a brief respite from his work.

"What do you give them?"

"They get a package deal. A pint of Guinness and six fresh oysters with homemade brown bread each. Sure, we hardly make anything from it, but it keeps us ticking over, and they're gone by three o'clock – long before the regulars come in."

Lyons let the man continue his task, and when he had placed all the cutlery he had in his hands, he went behind the bar and prepared three cups of coffee from a jar of instant. He filled a small jug with milk, and put the whole lot on a plastic tray and carried it across to where the Gardaí were seated.

As he put the tray down, he said, "And what brings you out this way today? We hardly ever see anyone in uniform in these parts."

Lyons took the sheet of A4 paper that she had in her jacket and unfolded the very unflattering photograph of the victim, holding it up for the proprietor to look at.

"Would you have seen this man here at all recently?" she said.

The man said nothing but walked away, back behind the bar.

Lyons looked at her two colleagues and shrugged, but the barman returned quickly enough, this time wearing a pair of glasses. He took the page from Lyons and looked at it carefully, twisting it left and right and squinting at the image.

"God help us, it's not much of a photograph, is it? His name is Terry Halpin. Looks like he's having a rough day – a very rough day."

"Terry Halpin. Is he a regular here?" Lyons asked.

"No, I wouldn't say that. But he's been in a few times, all right."

Fahy made a note of the name in her pocketbook.

"When was he in here last, ehhh …?"

"Sorry. It's Cathal, Cathal McDermott. Let me see now – ah, it must have been a week ago at least. I can't be sure of the day exactly. But about that, I'd say."

"And was he on his own?"

"No, not the last time he was in in any case. He was with another man, but I didn't recognise him at all. Not from around these parts."

"What did this other man look like?"

"Ah, ye know, kinda average. Brown hair, swarthy complexion – that's about it. We were fierce busy, so I didn't pay too much attention."

"And how do you know Terry Halpin, Cathal?" Fahy said.

"Sure, everyone knows Terry, don't they? He lives up in one of the bog cottages at Screebe with his mam and dad."

"Bog cottages?" Fahy said.

"God you lot must be right city girls, all right. Yeah. There was a scheme back in the 1950s to dig out the bog all around here and a string of eight cottages were built to house the workers. It never worked out of course, but ever since, them houses are called bog cottages. Terry's father bought his off the Turf Board back at the end of the seventies. They'd been left empty for ages after the turf thing went wrong, and they were in a poor state, but Halpin soon put his one right. I guess that's where Terry learned his trade."

"And what trade is that?" Fahy said.

"Handyman. He does a bit of plumbing, plastering, carpentry – you know the kind of thing. Anyway, listen, I'd best get on. This lot will be here in a few minutes."

"Just before you go, I don't suppose you have any CCTV here at all?" Lyons said.

"Jesus! You've been watching too much American TV. No, we don't have any of that stuff. We have a webcam that broadcasts the view out over the bay when the signal is up. It's pretty hit and miss. Some fella sold it to me a year or so ago, but I haven't seen him since – the chancer."

"Do you know if it records?"

"No, it doesn't. Just sends out pretty pictures. Apparently, some foreigners like to look at it. Now, I really must get on."

When McDermott had gone back to his preparations, Lyons said to Fahy, "Sally, give Eamon a call with that name will you, and see if he can come up with anything on him. Mary and I will go up to Screebe and see if we can find some of the Halpins. When we get back, we can all go down to the sea and look for anything that might be a bit out of place.

Chapter Five

Screebe was another township that was really only a crossroads. The junction itself was festooned with signs for several scenic locations in the area – The Wild Atlantic Way, the Pearse Visitors' Centre, and the ferry and tiny airport at Inverin that took visitors out to the Aran Islands.

It was 17km from Kilnatrá, and it took Lyons just twenty-five minutes to cover the distance on the narrow, undulating road. Just beyond the crossroads, the row of eight small cottages that the publican had described came into view. The two nearest to them were still unoccupied, and were boarded up. But the remaining cottages were refurbished. They were set back just five metres from the road, with a tiny grass patch in front of each, and a narrow wooden gate.

Lyons pulled the car into the side of the road and parked it half up on the verge.

"I wonder which is Halpin's?" she said.

"Who knows. But the fourth one along looks tidier than the others. Based on what McDermott said, I'd try that one first. What do you reckon?" Fahy said.

"Yeah, OK. Let's give it a try."

The two detectives got out of the car and approached the little cottage. It was freshly painted outside in white emulsion paint, and had a pillar box red front door, split in half horizontally, so that the top half could be opened to ventilate the place without letting pets or small children out onto the road.

The top half of the door was open, and swung gently in the light breeze.

Lyons knocked on the door. "Hello. Is anyone in?" she said, taking in the smell of fresh baking wafting out from inside.

The rest of the house looked as well-ordered as the outside, and a few moments later, a woman, dressed in a floral apron with tight grey curly hair shuffled across to the door, wringing her hands which she had just rinsed.

She looked surprised to see the two women, and not a little startled.

"Hello. Can I help you?" she said nervously.

"We're looking for the Halpins' place. Can you direct us to the right house?" Fahy said.

"I'm Mrs Halpin. Who are you?" The woman didn't mean to be rude, but she was quite taken aback by the presence of her visitors, and her instincts told her that they weren't delivering good news.

"Sorry, Mrs Halpin. I'm Detective Inspector Maureen Lyons and this is my colleague, Detective Sergeant Sally Fahy. May we come in for a moment?"

Mrs Halpin slipped the bolt securing the lower half of her front door and held it open. It led directly into the kitchen which had a flagged floor, a turf fired range, a white earthenware sink with a single cold tap above it, and a raw wooden table with four plain rail-backed chairs positioned around it. The accoutrements of baking, along with a bag of flour, a slab of margarine, a sieve and a large mixing bowl were on the table.

"You'll have to excuse the state of the place," the woman said apologetically, "I'm in the middle of baking some bread and scones."

"That's no problem, Mrs Halpin, we won't stay long. May I ask if you have a son called Terry?" Lyons said.

"Terry, yes, of course. Why? What's he done?"

"Is he around today at all?" Lyons said.

"No, no he's not. He hasn't been here for a few days now. I think he's got a job in the city doing up an old place. He'll be back at the weekend most likely – when he needs his clothes washed."

"Does he live here with you?" Fahy asked.

"Ah, sometimes. But he's more often than not in Galway these days, working. He shares a place with a friend of his."

"Mrs Halpin, I'm sorry to say we think your son may have been involved in an incident a few days ago."

"Incident – what kind of 'incident'?"

"May I ask you to have a look at this photograph. I'm afraid it's not very good, but maybe you will be able to recognize the person in it," Lyons said. She took the page out of her pocket, and for the second time that morning, unfolded it and showed it to the woman.

"Oh my God. That's our Terry. Is he… Is he… well you know?" she stammered.

Fahy moved around to be beside Mrs Halpin and helped her into one of the kitchen chairs.

"I'm afraid so. His body was recovered from the sea yesterday a good bit in nearer Galway. In fact, my Superintendent was the one who found him."

"Dear God. I always had a feeling he'd come to no good, but I never expected him to drown. Was he swimming or what?"

"Eh, no, Mrs Halpin. Terry was fully clothed when he was taken from the water. He hadn't been swimming. But we don't think he drowned either."

"What do you mean? I thought you said he was taken from the sea."

"He was, but he had an injury to the back of his head which we believe may have been the cause of his death."

No one said anything for a few minutes. When Lyons felt that the woman had had time to take in what she had been told, she said, "Can we get someone to come and be with you, Mrs Halpin? You've had a terrible shock."

"No, it's OK. Hugh will be back in half an hour or so. He's just gone over to O'Flynn's to help sort out some machine or other. I'll be fine. But, God, what do you think happened to the lad? He wasn't a bad boy really – he just got in tow with a rough lot when he was seventeen. He didn't deserve to be killed though."

"Can you tell us about his associates, Mrs Halpin? You mentioned that some of them were rough. Have you any names?"

"God, let me see. One of them he went around with was a Gillespie – Keith Gillespie. He came from somewhere out around Clifden, but I think he moved to Galway a couple of years back. And there was another lad too. Dunphy, I think his name was, but I can't remember his first name. But listen, what about the arrangements – you know. Can we see him?"

"Yes, of course. I'll arrange for someone to take you into Galway, maybe tomorrow morning, if that suits. Would that be OK?"

"Yes, I suppose so. Dear God, this is terrible. What are we going to do?"

Lyons recognised that there was no answer to the woman's question, so the two women made their excuses and left the little house, promising to be in touch later with the arrangements. Lyons knew from experience that you had to let this type of news settle.

And they would need to get one of them in to identify the body, which would be a dreadful experience for whichever of them decided to do it.

* * *

On the way back to Kilnatrá, Lyons asked Fahy to call Galway and give the names that Mrs Halpin had disclosed to Eamon Flynn so that he could start looking into Terry Halpin's known associates.

When Fahy had completed the call, Lyons said, "I'd better give Séan Mulholland a call too. See if he can find out anything about Keith Gillespie."

Lyons called the Garda station out in Clifden, and it was answered by Jim Dolan.

"Hi, Jim. Is Séan there? It's Maureen Lyons."

"Hello, Inspector. No, he's gone out for a while. He won't be long. Can I help at all?"

Lyons recited the details that they had been given by Terry Halpin's distraught mother, and asked him to start enquiries concerning Keith Gillespie.

By the time they had finished the phone calls, they were just coming back into Kilnatrá, where a 29-seater coach was now parked alongside Mary Fallon's Garda car. Mary was seated inside her vehicle nursing another cup of coffee in a large white mug. Lyons was amused by the fact that she had managed to get Cathal McDermott to prepare it for her, but Mary was a pretty girl with pale blonde hair that she wore in a ponytail, and bright blue eyes, and she wasn't beyond a little bit of flirting when the occasion demanded. It didn't surprise Lyons that McDermott had fallen for her charms.

Chapter Six

"Look at you!" Lyons said, smiling, when Mary Fallon opened the door of the squad car.

"Oh, hi, Inspector. Did you find the Halpins' place OK?"

"Yes, we did, and we got a bit of information about the deceased from his mother. I don't suppose you've ever come across a Keith Gillespie in your travels?" Lyons said.

"No, doesn't ring a bell – sorry."

"Never mind. I have Jim Dolan on the case now. Let's see if he can find out anything. Right, well, finish your drink and let's go down to the shore and see if we can see anything out of place."

The three women made their way across the car park, into a rocky field, and picked their way carefully down the steep, slippery ground to the sea. The coast was largely rocky in this location, and wet seaweed clinging to the boulders made moving around quite treacherous. Just where the Atlantic Ocean met the shore, there was a small patch of white sand – fine seashells that had been ground down by the constant motion of the waves. She took a plastic zip-lock bag from her pocket and scooped up a handful of the substance, much to the surprise of her colleagues.

"It's for comparison to the residue Dodd found in Halpin's shoes and socks. See if it came from the same place," Lyons said by way of explanation. "Have a good look around in the rock pools and in between the stones – see if there's any trace of anything that looks like it shouldn't be there."

The Gardaí made slow progress, given the difficult nature of the terrain, and several times whispered expletives could be heard as one or other of them immersed their feet into a chilly pool of sea water trapped in the crevices.

Just when they were about to call it a day, Mary gave a shout, "Over here! I've found something."

Lyons and Fahy scrambled over to where Mary Fallon was standing, looking down into a deep fissure.

"What is it Mary?" Fahy said.

"Looks like a trainer. Shall I lift it out?"

"No, leave it. I'll get it in a moment," Fahy said, putting on a pair of blue vinyl gloves and taking a large evidence bag out from her jacket pocket. Fahy bent down and tugged at the sodden shoe until it was dislodged, and placed it in the bag.

"Nice one, Mary. What do you do for an encore?" Lyons said.

"If we stay here long enough, maybe I could get a complete outfit," Fallon said smiling, but secretly she was quite pleased that as the junior officer she had found something of interest.

They spent another half an hour going back over the same area, but found nothing more other than a few empty beer cans and a broken bottle or two. Lyons collected the shards of glass and put them in yet another plastic bag, but this one was destined for the waste bin that McDermott had thoughtfully left at the side of the pub's car park.

When they got back to the area outside the hostelry, the mini-bus had departed.

"Right. OK, Mary. We'll get back into town. Thanks for coming out, and well done finding the shoe. Give Pascal our regards," Lyons said.

As Mary Fallon was bidding the other two farewell, and getting back into her own car, her mobile phone rang. It was Pascal Brosnan.

"Hi, Pascal. What's up?"

"Mary, where the hell are you? I've been trying to reach you. Is Inspector Lyons still with you?"

"I'm out at Kilnatrá, and yes, the Inspector and Sergeant Fahy are just leaving. Why?"

"Well don't let them go. Stop them."

Lyons was just pulling out of the car park, so Mary acted quickly and gave a couple of blasts on the car's siren and turned on the blue flashing lights. Lyons spotted them in her rear-view mirror and did a 360-degree turn, bringing her Volvo back alongside Mary's squad car.

"Everything OK, Mary?" Lyons said as she wound down the window.

"Pascal is on the phone. He wants to talk to you," Fallon said, handing the instrument to Lyons through the open window.

After Lyons ended the call, she said to Fahy, "Very mysterious. He wants us to come into Roundstone, but he wouldn't say why. But it sounded serious. C'mon. Let's go!"

* * *

They agreed that Mary should go first, so that if they encountered any traffic she could use her lights and sirens to get past the obstruction. Lyons followed, noting that Mary Fallon was no slouch behind the wheel as they picked up speed to over 80kph across the narrow, uneven bog road.

They arrived in Roundstone twenty-three minutes later, having shaved a full fifteen minutes off the recommended journey time, according to Google Maps. As they sped through the village, a few heads turned to observe the little convoy and the few locals that were out on the street wondered what was going on. There would be lots of gossip in the pubs later on.

* * *

"Well, Pascal, what's all the mystery about?" Lyons said as they entered the small, modern Garda station situated beside the church on the Clifden side of the village.

"Ah, come in, folks. Would you like a cup of tea? I have the kettle boiled."

"No, you're grand. Just tell us what's brought us here in such a hurry, will you?" Lyons said, beginning to lose patience with Brosnan's mysterious manner.

"You'd better sit down, Inspector."

Lyons and Fahy looked at each other and took a seat each in the office at the back of the station.

"One of the old timers was out and about earlier over by Lough Bollard. He has a few cattle that he's finishing for market in another couple of weeks, and he had gone out to see that they were all right. Just on the edge of the lake, behind one of the old ruined cottages, he came across a burnt-out van."

"Right," Lyons said.

"The vehicle was more or less totally destroyed, according to the old guy, but when he went to have a closer look, he found a body inside in it. The poor man got an awful fright, and he came straight in here on his old tractor to report it."

"Crikey! Is it recent, do you think?" Lyons said.

"Yes, I asked him that too, but he couldn't say. To be honest, I think he was in shock."

"I bet he was. So, what have you done so far, Pascal?" Lyons said.

"Well, I called it in to Sergeant Mulholland of course, and he's been on to Galway. They are sending out the forensic team – they should be here in a few minutes, and then we're going to go across to the van. I was hoping you could take charge, Inspector."

"Right. I see now why you didn't want to talk on the phone. OK, I'll take control. When the forensic team gets here, you can show us where this Lough Bollard is and how we get there. Is it far?" Lyons said.

"No. About ten minutes away, but when you turn off the main Clifden Road, it's only a wee narrow track. We'd better go in the 4x4 when it gets here."

Just as Brosnan was saying this, the large white Toyota Land Cruiser belonging to the Galway Forensic team pulled into the car park outside the Garda station. Lyons spotted Sinéad Loughran, whom she knew well from many other adventures, hopping down from the driver's seat in her usual cheerful, upbeat manner. Loughran was another pretty blonde girl that had become a friend of Lyons' some time ago. She was always bright and breezy, despite the fact that she had to deal with some very gruesome cases, and Lyons and herself frequently went for a drink and a natter after work when they were in the middle of some testing investigation. Lyons always felt better when Loughran was around.

"Hi, Maureen. Sally. I believe you have a cremation for me to examine!" Loughran said glibly.

"News travels fast, Sinéad. You don't have the lovely Dr Dodd with you then?"

"No, he's back at the mortuary. He'll get stuck in when we get whatever it is back to the city."

Lyons explained the nature of the grim discovery, and after a few minutes, Pascal left Mary Fallon in charge of the Garda station, and Loughran, Lyons, Fahy and himself set off in the Toyota for Lough Bollard.

* * *

"Here, turn right here onto the R311," Brosnan instructed as they slowed for a bad bend on the Roundstone to Clifden Road.

Loughran wheeled the big jeep onto the small track, and they slowed to 20kph as they bounced along over the rough ground towards the lake.

Lough Bollard is the English name for Loch Buaile Áird, which means the high dairy, although there was no sign of any such thing on this bright early summer day. There were one or two old deserted stone cottages along the track, with no rooves and weeds growing up enthusiastically all over, but no sign of anything that might have resembled commercial activity. A few sheep grazed lazily on the stunted grass between the rocky limestone outcrops, and as they approached the lake itself, they could see the small herd of tan-coloured cattle that the old farmer had been concerned about when he came across the burnt-out van.

The lake itself, swollen with the recent rains, was very picturesque. The Twelve Pins – that mountain range made famous by the artist Paul Henry – stood as a backdrop to the scene, and as the sun shone on the rippling surface of the water, it was hard to imagine a less likely place to find a corpse, let alone a crime scene.

Loughran slowly navigated the road, which had become nothing more than two stony ruts in the ground with a healthy crop of green weeds between them, and after another few minutes of bouncing around, she pulled the jeep up alongside an old derelict cottage.

"This must be the place," Brosnan said, opening the rear door of the Toyota and hopping out. He was quickly joined by the rest of them, and they walked around the old building, trying not to disturb the place too much in case there might be evidence concealed in the long grass and reeds.

As they rounded the corner of the ruin, there, tucked up tightly against what was once the side wall of the house, was the burnt-out van. Lyons and Fahy held back, and Loughran, once she had donned her blue overshoes, and fastened up her scene of crime suit, advanced on the wreck.

Fahy had brought some blue and white Garda tape with her, and was walking around in a wide circle, using whatever broken pieces of wood she could find to construct a rudimentary fence, and enclose the scene.

As Loughran began to probe the old van, she shouted back to Lyons, "See if you can see any tracks, Sally. Whoever did this hardly walked back to civilization."

Some seventy metres along the lane over which they had driven, there was some soft ground, and Lyons and Fahy walked back at the side of the path in the grass, so as not to disturb any possible evidence. When they got to the small patch of mud where there had been a large puddle left by the rain, Lyons bent down and examined the ground carefully.

"Look, Sally. We can see the marks from the jeep we came in. And these ones must be the van itself. But what about these ones. They're different. Mark this area with your tape, will you, and I'll get Sinéad to have a look when she's finished with the van."

Chapter Seven

When Sinéad Loughran had finished a thorough examination of the burnt-out van and its gory contents, she came back over to where Lyons and Fahy were sitting on a rock chatting to Pascal Brosnan.

"Well, what's the story, Sinéad?" Lyons asked.

Loughran unzipped the hood of her white suit and removed her vinyl gloves.

"A man in his late twenties or thirties, I'd say. He's only been here since yesterday, or last night. Diesel, probably from the fuel tank, was used to set the fire. The van was full of junk, so there was no trouble finding something combustible to get things going. I'd say he was already dead when he was set alight. He's laid out flat in the back of the van. If he'd been alive, he would have moved around a lot and struggled – maybe even got to the lake to extinguish himself."

"Any sign of injury ante mortem?" Lyons said.

"Jesus! Maureen, give me a chance. We'll have to get him back to Galway and let Dodd have a go at him to find that out."

"Oh, right, sorry. Listen, can you get the wagon out from the morgue to take the body back into Galway. Are you going to get anyone else out to help go over the scene?"

"Yes. I'll ask a couple of my team to come out in the van, and we'll do a proper search of the place and the surroundings," Loughran said.

"Great. Then, Pascal, when Sinéad has finished, could you get onto our old friend Deasy and get him to come and lift the van and bring it back to Roundstone. He can park it at the back of the station there. Are there any reg plates on it?"

"No, nothing. I'll have a look around in case whoever did this chucked them. They might even be in the lake," Brosnan said.

Tadgh Deasy ran a garage of sorts about two kilometres past Roundstone on the Recess road. He fixed up cars that were past repair at any of the main dealerships in Galway, and kept them going long after they should have been retired. He sold the odd vehicle from time to time too, and the Gardaí weren't too happy about the provenance of every car he put through his hands, but it suited them to keep him on side for occasions such as this.

"Yes, OK, boss. What are you going to do?" Brosnan said.

"I'm going to head on into Clifden and talk to Séan. We may need to set up an incident room in Roundstone. I'll call you as soon as I know what's going on. I'll get Mary to come out in my car as far as the junction with the main road, and you can give her a lift back in the jeep."

* * *

"Ah, come in, Maureen. I've just put the kettle on. Good timing," Mulholland said.

Séan Mulholland ran the Garda station in Clifden where he had a team of ten other officers to look after the area. He was a lone bachelor who lived in a rather scruffy house out on the Sky Road, and could have retired by now, except that he enjoyed the work and the camaraderie that his position afforded, and he would be at a dreadful loose end if he didn't have the job to keep him busy.

Mulholland was a man who was used to a gentler pace than the Gardaí were now attempting to impose on the entire force across the country, but the superintendent, recognising Mulholland's very considerable experience, left him more or less to his own devices, and to date it had worked out well.

"Thanks, Séan, that would be lovely. I suppose you've heard about the body in the van we found out by Lough Bollard," Lyons said.

"I did indeed. Do you think the two are connected?" Mulholland said, referring to the first body that Hays had fished out of the bay. He then went on to complete the preparations, and presented Lyons with a large mug of the strong hot tea, and the inevitable open packet of chocolate Goldgrain biscuits that were his signature any-time-of-day snack.

"Well, it would be some damn coincidence if there were two murders out here at the same time, wouldn't it?" Lyons said.

"Was the fella in the van murdered?"

Lyons went on to explain what they knew so far.

"Any ID on him?" Mulholland said taking a swig of tea and munching on a biscuit.

"Nothing obvious. The plates have been stripped from the van, but we may be able to get the VIN number off it and trace something that way."

Mulholland gave Lyons a sideways look.

"Have you told the superintendent yet?"

Mulholland wasn't completely convinced that female detectives were really up to the job. He had at one time been the same rank as Maureen Lyons, and they had worked together on a number of tricky cases where Lyons had more than proved her capabilities, but the old male bias was a strong instinct with the man who had spent the greater part of his career in an all-male environment.

"No, not yet. I think he's pretty tied up today. I'll bring him up to speed when I get back to Mill Street. Is there any gossip going around out here about Terry Halpin yet?"

"Oh, that one. Not that I've heard – not yet anyways. But I'll be in Cusheen's later, and I'll keep me ears pinned back."

Cusheen's was the pub that Mulholland liked to frequent after work to drink a few pints of Guinness while he read the paper sitting at the open turf fire. It was a rather basic establishment, with a flagged floor and old, well-worn wooden furniture, but it suited Mulholland, and he often picked up scraps of useful information from eavesdropping on the locals as he sat quietly in his favourite spot, reading the paper and ostensibly minding his own business.

"Right, well we need to start some enquiries into the Halpin killing anyway. Can you get Jim and Peadar out to do the door-to-door stuff around Kilnatrá. McDermott said he had been in the pub with another man some time before he died. We need to find out who that was, and if possible, what they were talking about. And keep Pascal on his toes too. Get him to mix it up a bit in Roundstone – see what he can find out.

"I will. I'm not keen on that Cathal McDermott," Mulholland said.

"Oh. Why's that?"

"Ah, it's nothing you could put your finger on, but he's shifty – very shifty."

"Have you ever got Customs and Excise to do an audit on him?"

"No, I haven't. I suppose it's hard enough to make a living stuck out there in the sticks, and there's very little trade in the winter months. Better to leave him alone and keep an eye on him, if you ask me."

"Maybe. When all this is over, we'll have another chat about that though," Lyons said.

"Right you are," Mulholland said.

"OK, well I'd better be getting back into town. Thanks for the tea, and be sure to let me know if you uncover any information, Séan."

"I will that. Mind the road then, and give my regards to the superintendent."

Chapter Eight

It was late afternoon by the time Lyons got back to the Garda station at Mill Street. She had stopped in Roundstone on the way back and spoken to Mary Fallon to ensure that herself and Pascal were fully engaged in the investigation. Brosnan still wasn't back from Lough Bollard, but Mary had been talking to him, and had been told that the body had left to go to Galway, and that Deasy was lifting what remained of the van back to the Garda station.

Back in her office, she tried to contact Mick Hays, but his secretary told her that he was still out at a meeting, but was expected back shortly.

She was just updating the Garda PULSE system with the latest information when her phone rang.

"Lyons."

"Inspector, this is Dr Dodd. I have a bone to pick with you."

"Oh, how's that, Doc?"

"I should have been called out to Lough Bollard to examine the body of this specimen you've had delivered to me. God knows what contamination has taken place, and he's been moved around a lot too during transportation."

"I'm sorry, Doctor. I thought you wouldn't relish a trip out to a boggy marsh in the middle of the working day. Anyway, what can you tell me about the body?" Lyons said, not allowing herself to be put off by the man's attitude.

"Really, Inspector, it's not good enough. In future, I at least need to be consulted in these matters. I *am* the appointed state pathologist, after all."

Lyons thought he must be having a really bad day. It wasn't like him to be quite so grumpy. Superior – yes, but usually fairly cheerful. And she didn't want to get her pal Sinéad into trouble either – after all it was Sinéad's idea not to call him out.

"Yes, I'm sorry, Doctor. I'll remember in future. Anyway, what can you tell me about the man?"

"Please do! Nothing as yet. Male, probably early thirties. I'm just getting started on him – I'll let you know a bit later when I can untangle this mess. Fancy coming over to watch me work on him?"

"Eh... no thanks, I'll pass on that one. But please do let me know whatever you find as soon as you have it. I don't want the trail going cold."

"Naturally," Dodd said, and hung up without bidding Lyons goodbye.

Lyons held the telephone receiver away from her face and looked at it curiously.

"Who's been rattling your cage then, Doc?"

She had just put the phone down, when it rang again.

"Hi. It's me. You were looking for me," Hays said.

"Oh, hi. Yes, I wanted to bring you up to date with what's been going on out in the west."

"Look, love, I'm up to my elbows in bloody spreadsheets and reports for Plunkett. He has some big meeting on tomorrow and he wants to have lots of data that no one will read in any case. Can we leave it till later?"

"Mm... OK. How much later?" Lyons said.

"Give me an hour. Let's meet at O'Connaire's for food. Will you book it for, say, seven?"

"Yes, OK. See you there."

Hays hung up.

"Must be something in the water today," she said to herself.

* * *

O'Connaire's was a fashionable bistro overlooking the harbour down by the docks in Galway city. It was one of Hays and Lyons' favourite places to eat, and as they were frequent patrons, they were given priority when it came to getting a reservation on a busy evening.

It was bustling as usual when Lyons arrived and was shown to a table for two on the upper floor adjacent to a window overlooking the quays. She explained to the very attentive young waitress that she was awaiting her partner, and ordered a glass of chardonnay to help pass the time.

It was all of twenty past seven when Hays came clumping up the bare wooden stairs, and joined Lyons, giving her a perfunctory kiss on the cheek before taking his seat.

"God! What a day that was. Yer man is going nuts. Apparently, we're over budget on overtime again, and he'd given an undertaking last quarter that he would rein things in. So he's all set for a roasting tomorrow up in The Park," Hays said.

Lyons said nothing. She knew enough about her partner to let him vent before saying anything. He didn't really want a response in any case. He went on about the work he had been doing for another few minutes, then sat back, and took a deep breath.

"Sorry, love. It's just all this administration drives me mad. And no one pays any attention to the results in any case – except to take a few lumps out of Plunkett to keep him on the straight and narrow."

"What you need, Superintendent, is a woman's touch," Lyons said.

Hays smiled.

"What do you mean?"

"Well, If I was in charge, the overtime figures would come in exactly on budget, and whatever excess needed to be dealt with would go into cleaning, maintenance or vehicle repairs, or some other heading that can't be argued about."

"Don't think I haven't thought of that. It's only by means of some 'adjustments' that we're not a lot worse off. Anyway, never mind all that. What have you been up to?"

Lyons told Hays about the burnt-out remains in the van, and told him about the developments concerning the body he had encountered out sailing.

"Wow! Talk about having your hands full. Any useful leads?"

"No. None. The first thing we need to establish is if the two events are connected. Seem like a very big coincidence to have two suspicious deaths in that area at the same time. But we haven't a clue who the second one is yet."

"I'm sure you'll make progress over the next few days."

Just then, their waitress, Aisling, arrived at the table with menus.

"Good evening folks. How are you both?" she said cheerily.

"Hungry," Hays replied.

"Well, we have some really nice fresh turbot on tonight. I saw it in the kitchen earlier – it's huge."

"Sounds good. I'll have that please, Aisling," Lyons said.

"I feel like something a bit more substantial, Aisling. What's good?" Hays said.

"Chef says he has some really nice venison, Mr Hays. It's not on the menu, but he has two lovely steaks you could have."

"Perfect! And some of those fabulous game chips he does too. Excellent – thanks."

Aisling scribbled down the orders on her little notepad.

"Are you OK for drinks?" she said.

Lyons was still nursing the glass of wine from earlier, so she said she didn't need anything more.

"Could you send out a nice glass of Rioja with the meal, Aisling?"

"Sure, no problem. I'll get you some bread while you're waiting."

Their meal was sumptuous, and they took their time over it, finishing with the cheese board which was always exceptional at O'Connaire's.

"Leave your car here if you like," Hays said as they left the restaurant, "we can pick it up in the morning on the way in."

"Nah, it's OK. I've only had the one glass of wine, and I'd prefer to have the car at home in case something develops during the night."

"OK. Well, see you in a few minutes," Hays said and leaned in and gave Lyons a quick kiss on the cheek.

* * *

Lyons' car was facing south on Claddagh Quay, so she decided to go home via Grattan Road. It would only add a minute or so to the journey, but she couldn't be bothered trying to turn the car around on the narrow quayside. She was just approaching the Fairhill Road junction when a uniformed Garda in a yellow high-viz jacket stepped out in front of her car with his hand up. Lyons stopped and wound down the window. She didn't recognize the officer, who was young and fresh-faced and obviously from an out-of-town station.

"Good evening, ma'am. May I see your driver's license please?" the young man said, leaning down and looking in the window.

"Yes, of course, officer. It's here in my handbag," Lyons said, reaching across to the passenger's seat and withdrawing her wallet. Her driving license was displayed in a clear plastic section, and there was a corresponding see-through panel on the other side that contained her warrant card.

The young Garda took the wallet and inspected it.

"Thank you, that seems to be in order. May I ask if you've had a drink at all this evening?" the man enquired, smelling a slight whiff of alcohol through the open window.

"Yes, Guard, I had one glass of wine with my meal about forty-five minutes ago."

The young man smiled slightly. There was nothing that some of these eager new recruits liked more than to catch a senior officer driving under the influence. It was worth endless banter amongst their colleagues, and was considered a rite of passage for many of them.

"I'm afraid I'm going to have to ask you to take a breath test, ma'am," he said, standing up to unclip the equipment from his belt. He removed a single-use plastic mouthpiece from its cellophane wrapping and fixed it into the small black hand-held device offering it to Lyons and instructing her to keep blowing into it until it beeped.

"Yes, Guard, I know how these things work," Lyons said sourly.

She put the tube in her mouth and blew until the machine issued a long high-pitched sound, and handed it back to the officer, who was disappointed to see that it had registered below the drink-driving limit.

"Thank you, Inspector, that's fine. You can be on your way now," he said, standing back from the car and waving her on.

Lyons had noted the shoulder number of the young officer. It was a GA divisional badge, but that meant that he could have been from any station from Clifden to

Ballinasloe – but she had memorised the number too, so she would find out exactly where he was based.

Chapter Nine

Lyons arrived at Mill Street early the following morning and found Sally Fahy and Eamon Flynn already at their desks.

"Morning all. I just want to get a cup of coffee, and then we'll get together for a briefing. Ask John to join us, Eamon."

John O'Connor was a young uniformed Garda who had been assigned to the detective unit on account of his keen interest and considerable skill with technology. He enjoyed working with PCs, mobile phones, CCTV and any other form of gadget that cropped up in the course of an investigation. He had contributed significantly to several of the cases that Lyons had been involved with, and was held in high regard by the rest of the team.

"OK, boss."

Lyons went to the back of the open plan and boiled up the kettle, putting a spoon of instant coffee granules into her favourite mug. As she was pouring in the hot liquid, Sally Fahy came across to join her.

"Hi, Sally. Coffee?" Lyons said.

"No, I've just had one, thanks. Did the superintendent have any ideas about this lot out in Kilnatrá?"

"We had a chat about it last night, all right. But he's just as puzzled as we are so far. But you know his mantra – 'follow the money'."

"Hmm... he's probably right. Dr Dodd's preliminary report on Halpin is in. Nothing very surprising, but I gave Sinéad a quick call and asked her for the real low down."

"Anything?" Lyons said.

"She just said that Halpin's clothes were pretty expensive. That jacket was Tommy Hilfiger – would have cost a few hundred euro, and the rest of his gear was much the same. Seems a bit odd for a handyman, don't you think?"

They took their drinks back to the centre of the room where the rest of the team had assembled. Lyons stood at the front of the group, adjacent to the whiteboard that bore a picture of the deceased and a detailed map of the location.

"Right, plans for the day. Eamon, will you take Dermot and start work on the body in the van? We need to identify the deceased as a matter of priority. See if you can find out who owns the vehicle. Then hook up with Pascal and see if anyone has seen it around. And follow up with Dodd to see what he's been able to do with the burnt body. Any luck with those names I gave you yesterday – what was it – Gillespie and Dunphy?"

"Not yet, boss. I have some feelers out though," Flynn said.

"Sally. Will you get working on Terry Halpin. You know, all the usual. Social Security records, any previous we might have on him. Then get John onto his mobile phone, social media presence and bank accounts. When you have arranged all that, find out where he was staying in Galway and who with. By the end of the day, I want us to know more about him than he knew himself. Let's reconvene at five or whatever time we're all back in and compare notes."

"What are you going to do, boss?" Fahy said.

"I'm going to take Mary back out to the Halpins' house and ask them some questions. I want to get more information on his known associates from them, and have a look at his room. Eamon, what would you think if we asked Mary Fallon to act as FLO for the Halpins? She might pick up some useful information."

"Sounds about right. Would Pascal be OK on his own for a few days?" Flynn said.

"I reckon so. She's had the training, and she's smart, so it could come in handy."

* * *

Lyons called Roundstone and spoke to Pascal Brosnan, who was happy to donate his only officer to the cause for a few days. Lyons arranged to meet Mary Fallon at Screebe close to the Halpins' house.

Lyons took the coast road from the city through Salthill where she shared a house with her life partner, and on to Barna, Furbo and Spiddal. Although it was a bright day, it was windy, and the Atlantic Ocean bore a covering of white tops to the waves as she drove along by the sea. At Inverin the road turned north to bring her up past Costello and finally into Screebe. She arrived at the little cottage at quarter past ten where Mary Fallon was waiting unobtrusively in her parked car some 200 metres back from the cottage, and was surprised to find that the little house was full of people. But Fallon explained that that was the country way. The Halpins would not be left alone for a single minute until well after the funeral of their son, and much whiskey would be consumed along with endless sandwiches and cakes in the little homestead over the next several days.

A tall, sunburnt man in his late fifties, dressed in a grey T-shirt and baggy blue jeans, holding a generous measure of amber liquid in a tumbler appeared to dominate the group, and Lyons assumed that he was Hugh Halpin – father of the young man that had been pulled from the sea.

She slipped into the crowded kitchen and sidled up to the man.

"Mr Halpin?"

"Yes."

"I'm Detective Inspector Lyons from Galway, I wonder if we could have a word outside?"

Hugh Halpin looked around the room, as if to see that all his guests were well provisioned, put down his glass on the dresser and replied, "Yes, sure," gesturing towards the open door.

Outside, Lyons introduced Mary Fallon, and the three of them strolled around to the side of the house, out of sight of the front of the cottage.

"Mr Halpin, I'm very sorry for your loss. This is very tragic, and I'm sorry to bother you at a time like this, but we need to ask a few questions about Terry, if that's all right."

"Yes, I understand you have a job to do. But please don't bother my wife if you don't mind. She's destroyed by this."

"Can you tell us what exactly Terry was doing work-wise at the moment?" Lyons said, without providing any reassurance about Mrs Halpin to the man.

"He was working in Galway renovating property. They are doing it up. Terry said it was in a right old state."

"When you say 'they', Mr Halpin, who do you mean?"

"Ah, himself and that waster Keith Gillespie. I don't rate him much as a builder. Terry was doing most of the work, but he wasn't getting much of the money."

"I see. And where is this job located, Mr Halpin?" Fallon asked.

"It's on Market Street in the city. It's a terraced place that opens onto the street. It'll be grand when it's finished – but I suppose that might not happen now."

"Who owns it?" Fallon said.

"Some fella by the name of McGuire. He's a Northern Ireland man. I don't know what he's doing buying places in Galway, but apparently he has a few houses round and about."

Fallon made a note of the name in her pocketbook.

"What can you tell us about Keith Gillespie?" Lyons asked.

Hugh Halpin grunted out loud. "I wouldn't piss on him if he was on fire!"

"Oh, why's that?" Lyons said.

"He's a taker. Take, take, take and gives nothing back. He had poor Terry running around after him like a man-servant. I told Terry often enough to ditch him, but for some reason, he was caught under Gillespie's spell. And, sure, what young man takes any notice of what their father says in any case?"

"Where was Terry staying in the city, Mr Halpin?" Mary Fallon said.

"He was bunking down with Gillespie. Some bit of a place above a shop, wasn't it?"

"Do you know what the shop was called, or what number it was?"

"No, I don't. The shop was boarded up. A right dump, if you ask me."

"OK, thanks, Mr Halpin. That's very helpful. Do you know if Terry had a mobile phone and a laptop computer?" Lyons asked.

"He did of course! What young fella would be without those things these days?"

"Did he keep the laptop here?"

"No, he didn't. You'll probably find it in the bedsit, if Gillespie hasn't sold it by now."

"OK. Well thanks very much for your help, Mr Halpin. We won't disturb you anymore. You can get back to your guests. At some stage we'd like to come out and have a look at Terry's room, if that would be OK, but not today?"

"Yes, of course. But leave it a few days. This crowd will be gone in a day or two and then it'll just be me and the missus left to mourn the lad, won't it?"

"Yes, of course, and I've asked Mary here to be your family liaison officer – so anything you need or any questions you have, Mary will help you out. She'll be dropping in on you every day for the next week or so, if that's OK?"

"Oh, all right. But we might not be very hospitable," Halpin said.

"Don't worry – it's not hospitality I'm looking for. I just want to help in any way I can, and help you with the arrangements and so on," Mary said.

Lyons decided not to intrude further on the family's grief, and walked back to Fallon's car with the young Garda.

"Can you come back into town with me, Mary? We need as many people as we can get on this. I want to find this Gillespie character, and Mr McGuire."

"Sure. I'll just give Pascal a call and see that he's OK managing out at Roundstone, and then I'll follow you in."

"Right. Thanks."

When Lyons was back in her own car, she called Eamon Flynn and gave him the information about the site that Terry Halpin had been working on, and the details of the place where his father had said he was staying.

"Get round there, Eamon, and see if you can find anything of interest. And then see if you can locate Gillespie. Bring him in. I want to give him a good grilling. Any word from Dodd about the mysterious body in the van?"

"No, nothing yet. I'll get someone to give him a nudge."

"And any word on the van itself? Surely, we must have been able to identify it at least by now," Lyons said, trying not to let her frustration show too much.

"John is on it. It's not registered in the south in any case, so he's on to the PSNI and the DVLA with the VIN number to see what he can get. It will take you an hour to get back to town. Where do you want to meet?" Flynn said.

"Back at the station. But ring me if you have Gillespie, will you?"

"Righto, boss. See you later."

Chapter Ten

Sally Fahy was pleased to get a break from the desk work exploring all of the state's connections to the dead man when Eamon Flynn asked her to accompany him to the two locations Lyons had discussed.

"We'll start at the place they were doing up. Maybe we can lift Keith Gillespie there. Then we'll have a go at Halpin's digs."

Flynn and Fahy decided to walk to Market Street. It would give them the element of surprise that couldn't be afforded by a squad car in the narrow thoroughfare, and they just might be able to nab Keith Gillespie unawares in case he had any notion of making a run for it.

They walked down Mill Street and onto Bridge Street before crossing the River Corrib and turning left at the roundabout onto Market Street. Market Street was a strange mixture of very old and quite new buildings, housing all sorts of commercial enterprises and a few domestic dwellings. Down near the end of it, close to the junction with Abbeygate Street, they came across what they believed to be the premises that Mr Halpin had told them Terry was working on. There was a skip parked half up on the narrow footpath outside, and it was two-thirds full of old plasterboard, a rusty kitchen sink and some vitreous ware that had seen better days before being ripped out of the property. The front door had at one time been half-glazed, but now a roughly cut square of orange-coloured fibreboard occupied the top half of the entrance where glass had once been. The door itself, with its peeling red paint, was closed over, but had been left ajar.

Flynn looked at Fahy and gestured towards the partially closed door.

Fahy nodded, and Flynn knocked firmly on the wooden panel as he pushed the door open, shouting, "Hello. Is anyone in there?"

There was no reply, and a few moments later the two of them entered the premises, which was dark, and smelled musty and damp.

Flynn signalled Fahy to go into the room on the right of the hallway, while he started up the stairs. The floorboards creaked underfoot, and as Flynn ascended, he could see some light coming from a room on the right of the landing. He called out again, "Hello, is anyone there?"

Again there was no response, so he cautiously stepped towards the room where the light was coming from and pushed the door fully open so that it swung back almost flat against the wall in case there was someone concealed behind it. But the room was empty. A single electric bulb hung from the ceiling, shedding a dim light on the room which was in the very early stages of renovation. Some of the floorboards were missing, wallpaper was hanging down, and the window that gave onto the street below was shuttered from inside.

Flynn quickly checked the other two rooms off the landing, and found them to be in much the same condition. In the bathroom, now stripped of toilet, sink and bath, a toolbox lay open on the floor with various instruments of trade spilling out onto the floor.

The third room, which hadn't been molested as yet, was dark and dingy with an old bedstead and a filthy mattress stuck in the middle of the floor.

Flynn returned to the landing and shouted to his colleague.

"Sally. Anything downstairs?"

"No. Not a whisper," she said emerging back into the hall. "It's like the Mary Celeste!"

"OK," he said descending the stairs cautiously, "can you go next door and see if anyone knows where we can contact this McGuire character? I'll have another look around here."

"Right. Back in a minute," she said, letting herself out onto the street where the air was less fetid.

Flynn checked the back of the house where some new materials were stacked up waiting for the tradesmen to deploy them around the property, but there was no sign of life.

A few minutes later, the two detectives met up on the street.

"Did you get any info on McGuire?" Flynn said.

"Yes. I got an address for him. He has an office in Dominick Street. Do you want to go around there and see if he's in?"

"Not yet. We'd better check out the address in Eyre Street first. I'm sure Mr McGuire will keep for half an hour or so."

* * *

It took the two detectives just five minutes to cover the distance to Eyre Street, walking along Abbeygate Street and then into Mary Street. Eyre Street was similar in character to Market Street. On one side, commercial undertakings, and even some brand-named department stores offered their wares from brightly lit modernised premises, while on the other side of the narrow street terraces of small, two-storey cottages all in good condition and recently painted stood along the footpath. All of the shops seemed to be thriving, and there was a busy feel about the place. But down near the end of the street they could see a 'For Lease' sign suspended out above a boarded-up shop, claiming that the property could be used for a variety of different purposes.

"This must be it, Sally," Flynn said, "it's the only empty one I can see."

They approached the front of the building and saw that there was a door to the side of the steel shutters protecting the shop, which presumably led to the upstairs where Terry Halpin had been staying, according to his father.

Flynn pressed the doorbell fixed to the door-jamb. There was no name in the little plastic window that comprised the fitting, but they could hear a bell ringing inside. After a few minutes, when there was no reply, Flynn rang the bell again, this time keeping his finger on the little white button for quite some time.

"Dozy buggers are still probably asleep. Look, just in case, will you see if there's a rear entrance to this place. I don't want chummy doing a runner if he is inside."

"Yeah, sure. Give me a few minutes before you go in."

Fahy walked further up the street till she found a narrow alley along the side of the shops, and set off down it. At the end of the narrow passage, a laneway that ran behind the commercial premises was littered with all sorts of bins and a good deal of discarded cardboard and polystyrene packaging. Helpfully, the estate agent who was trying to rent the place that was boarded up had put a sign in the laneway too. There was a wooden door leading off the lane into the backyard of the old shop, and Fahy observed that it was almost totally overgrown with weeds and buddleia, sprouting bright purple flowers. She pushed the door which opened roughly, scraping along the uneven concrete, and let herself in.

She could see that a rusty set of iron stairs had been erected leading from a wooden door in the flat above the shop. The door was glazed and its paint, which had at one time been white, was now discoloured and peeling. The glass in the door was cracked, but not broken, and the whole place was extremely dirty, covered in dust and grime brought down by the frequent rain.

"God, the places some people live. This is a shithole!" she said to herself.

When Flynn had calculated that his colleague was positioned at the back of the place, he rang the bell one more time.

"Probable cause – here goes," he said, using the age old excuse that there could be someone injured inside the flat to force his way in through the door. As it transpired, the door yielded readily to his shoulder, and within a couple of seconds he was in, mostly unobserved by disinterested shoppers.

A creaky wooden stairs, which at one time had been carpeted but was now bare, led up from the front door to a small landing above. There were three doors off the landing, one of which stood open revealing a dirty bathroom with a filthy basin, toilet and bath. There was cracked linoleum on the floor and the basin had clearly been leaking, as there were brown stains going from its underside to a wet patch beneath.

"Is there anyone here?" Flynn said loudly to no response. He pushed open the door on the left of the landing and found himself looking into a bedroom. There were two single beds in the room with a cheap melamine locker between them, and a wardrobe which had at one time been flat-packed, but now stood at a rather strange angle with its door hanging open. An ancient floral carpet, threadbare in places, adorned the floor. There were sheets and duvets on the beds which were not made up, and these too looked as if they hadn't seen a washing machine for some time. The air was stale and musty.

The other room was a kitchen of sorts. An old cream-coloured gas cooker, a newer microwave and a dirty white plastic electric kettle took up most of the space, except for the steel sink positioned against the back wall beside the exit to the outside.

Flynn went to the door and tapped on the glass, signalling Fahy to re-join him.

When Fahy was back inside the flat, they both donned blue vinyl gloves and started a quick search. Under a pile of dirty clothes in the bedroom, Fahy came across a small backpack. It was new and clean, and looked out of place amongst the general detritus.

"Oi oi. What have we here?" she called out.

Flynn came across and they opened the bag. Inside, wrapped in clear plastic, were bundles of euro notes.

"Wow! Must be a couple of grand here at least," exclaimed Fahy.

"You'd better call it in, Sally. We need forensics around here with the team to give the place the once over, and one of us had better stay here in case someone comes back. Can you go around to McGuire's and see what he has to say? I'll hang on here," Flynn said.

"Yeah, OK. Will you be all right though? What if someone comes back and finds you in here? It could get rough."

Flynn smiled.

"Yes, it could – for them!"

Chapter Eleven

When Sally Fahy had called Sinéad Loughran and made the arrangements, she left her colleague to it and set off for Dominick Street. The street was narrow, like many of the streets in the city centre, and was populated by several restaurants, bars and take-away food shops of every size and style. There was even a tapas bar, possibly attracted to the location by the proximity of the Spanish Arch, a well-known landmark which originally formed part of the city walls erected in 1584. The arches themselves were cut through the old walls later by the Eyre family, but had been partly destroyed in 1755 by the tsunami that resulted from the Lisbon earthquake. More recently, they had been occupied by a civic museum.

Fahy walked along Dominick Street and soon found a pale green door sandwiched in between a hardware shop and yet another restaurant with a brass plate identifying the entrance as belonging to McGuire Enterprises. There was an intercom arrangement which Fahy used, and a moment later a female voice answered with the one word greeting, "Yes?"

Fahy announced herself and the door buzzed, allowing her to enter. The offices of McGuire Enterprises were on the first floor above the restaurant, but unlike the properties on Market Street and Eyre Street, this place was in very good repair. The walls on the stairway had been recently painted a neutral grey colour, and there was a fresh grey woollen carpet on the stairs and a highly polished handrail.

At the top of the stairs, a door marked 'Reception' stood open, and the tempting aroma of freshly made coffee wafted out onto the landing.

Fahy entered to find a young dark-haired girl with striking green eyes sitting behind a modern desk with a fancy-looking Apple iMac in front of her.

"Good morning," the girl said in a local, but refined, accent, "how can I help?"

"I was hoping to have a quick word with Mr McGuire if he's in," Fahy said, looking around and taking in the surroundings.

"Have you an appointment?"

"No, I'm afraid not, but it's quite important," she said, extending her warrant card in case the girl had missed the fact that she was from the police when she announced herself at the front door.

The girl said nothing, but lifted the phone on her desk and made a call, turning away from Fahy so that she couldn't hear the muted conversation.

"Mr McGuire will be with you in a moment. Would you like a cup of coffee?" the girl said, her demeanour much improved, no doubt on instruction from her boss.

"Yes, please. That would be lovely. Just a drop of milk – no sugar," Fahy said.

The girl turned around and inserted a capsule into the complicated-looking coffee machine on a shelf behind her, and almost at once it started gurgling and hissing, finally filling a mug with dark brown liquid with a paler froth on top. Milk was added, and the drink was given to Fahy who thanked her.

A door opened at the end of the reception area, and a smallish plump man dressed in a business suit with an open-necked shirt appeared. He had a swarthy complexion, dark greasy hair and spoke with a distinct Northern Ireland accent.

"Good morning, Detective, won't you come in?" he said as he stood aside and gestured for Fahy to go into his office. The office was small, but like the rest of the facility, was in immaculate order. An expensive modern desk with just a few manila files occupied about a third of the space, with a set of bookshelves, a low cabinet, and a few leather and chrome office chairs took up much of the rest. McGuire gestured again to Fahy to take a seat, and provided a coaster for her to rest her mug of coffee on at the front of his desk.

"Well now, what about ye?"

Fahy was good with accents. She knew at once that McGuire was not from Belfast – his voice was softer and more rounded than the harsh tones associated with Northern Ireland's capital city. More like Derry or Tyrone, she thought to herself as she took her seat in front of the man.

"Mr McGuire, may I ask if you know a lad called Terry Halpin?"

McGuire looked thoughtful for a moment, as if he was processing the request.

"Aye, I do. He does some work for me now and again, except that he hasn't turned up for the last week. Why? What about him?"

"What was he doing for you?" Fahy said.

"He was doing some building work for me down in Market Street. I have a place there that needs a bit of attention," McGuire said.

"I see. And is that place on Eyre Street yours too? You know, where Keith Gillespie was staying?"

"Yes, that's mine. It's next on the list for a makeover when Market Street is fixed up and re-let."

"Do you have many men like Halpin and Gillespie working for you, Mr McGuire?"

"Aye. It varies as the work comes and goes, you know."

Fahy decided not to mention PRSI and income tax just yet. She wanted to draw McGuire out a bit more first.

"Anyway, do you know where Halpin is, Sergeant? I need him back to finish off that place. I'll have a tenant for it soon."

"Mr McGuire, I'm sorry to have to tell you, but Terry Halpin is in the city morgue. He was pulled out of the sea last Sunday. We're investigating his death."

McGuire paled noticeably before recovering his composure.

"God, that's terrible. Poor lad. Had he gone swimming or something? Got out of his depth?"

"That's what we are looking into, Mr McGuire. Can you tell me if you own a white Ford Transit van?"

"I do – like every other builder in Ireland, I imagine. Why do you ask?"

"Where is the van now?"

"I suppose one of the men has it. Maybe even Gillespie. I don't keep track of every vehicle every day, Sergeant, I have too much going on for that."

"Have you just the one white van?"

"Aye. We have a few pick-up trucks too, and a JCB and a dumper as well."

"I wonder if I could have the registration details of the van?" Fahy said.

"I suppose so. Fionnula will get it for you, but why all the interest in the van?"

"Just following enquiries, sir. If you hear anything from Keith Gillespie, you might let us know. We're anxious to speak to him about Terry Halpin," Fahy said handing over her business card.

"Oh, right. Yes, will do."

Fahy got up to leave and McGuire ushered her back out into the reception area asking Fionnula to dig out the registration details of the Transit and give them to Fahy. When she got them in her hand, she noted that the van was still registered in Northern Ireland, but didn't say anything.

Chapter Twelve

It was approaching lunchtime when Lyons arrived back into Mill Street with Mary Fallon in tow.

"Why don't you nip out and get us both a nice sandwich and a coffee before we get stuck in, Mary? There's a little café just along the street," Lyons said, handing the junior officer a €20 note.

"OK. What do you fancy?"

"Whatever looks tasty – I'm not fussy."

Mary Fallon went off down the street while Lyons went back into the Garda station.

Upstairs in the open plan, John O'Connor was the only one present.

"Hi, John. Any news on anything?" Lyons asked.

"Hi, Inspector. Not a lot. I have the details of the white van. It's actually English. Last known keeper a courier service in Northampton. Then it was written off following a front end crash, and guess what – it turns up out here with us."

"Any idea who was using it now?"

"No, none, I'm afraid. It hasn't been taxed since the write-off, but I have the reg number. We could see if it's been picked up anywhere around for any reason."

"Yes, OK, do that. And talk to the others as well. They may have found out something about it."

"Oh, and Dr Dodd wants you to call him. He rang about twenty minutes ago."

"Right, thanks. I'll give him a ring now."

Lyons was just about to call the pathologist back in her office when her own phone sprung to life.

"Lyons."

"Hello, Inspector, it's Danny here at the front desk. There's a girl here says she wants to speak to someone about Terry Halpin. She's in a bit of a state. Could you send someone down maybe?"

"Yes, OK, Danny. What's her name?"

"Teresa Doyle."

"Right. I'll come down myself. Keep her there."

Teresa Doyle was a girl in her very late teens or early twenties. She had a shock of long red hair, which looked natural, as it went with her pale skin and the freckles that covered much of her face. She was slim, around 170 cm tall and was smartly dressed in well-fitting blue jeans and a green zip-through fleece over a polo shirt of matching colour.

"Hello, Teresa. My name is Senior Inspector Lyons. How can I help you?" Lyons said, extending her hand to greet the girl.

"Where is he? I want to know what you've done with him!" she said in an agitated manner.

"Where is who, Teresa?"

"Terry of course. Terry Halpin. His father told me to come here and you'd tell me."

"Teresa, let's go somewhere a bit more private and have a chat. I'll explain everything."

The girl remained quiet and allowed Lyons to usher her into one of the side rooms off the main public area. When they were both seated across the plain grey table, Lyons said, "Now, Teresa, may I ask what your connection is to Terry Halpin?"

"He's my boyfriend, and I want to know what you've done with him!"

"When did you last see Terry?"

"Two weeks ago. I've been in Ibiza with some mates. I just got back today, and telephoned him from the airport. But when I got no reply, I called his home and Mr Halpin told me to come here. What's going on?"

Lyons realized she couldn't hold off telling the girl what had happened for much longer, though she would have liked to get more information from her before the inevitable clamming up that normally came immediately after very bad news.

"I'm sorry to tell you, Teresa, but Terry has been involved in a very serious incident. We pulled him out of the bay last Sunday, and I'm sorry, but he didn't survive."

Teresa Doyle looked at Lyons for a long moment, and then said, "No. You can't have. Terry hated the water. He never went swimming or anything. There must be some mistake. That's not my Terry."

"I'm sorry, Teresa, there's no mistake. He's been identified."

The girl's head sank to her chest and she started sobbing uncontrollably. Lyons pushed the box of tissues that was a fixture in the little interview room towards her and Teresa took a few sheets and dabbed her eyes and nose.

"We've only been going out a few months – but I really liked him. Terry was a lovely guy. What happened to him?"

"We don't know yet, Teresa, but I can say that he didn't drown."

"I don't understand. You said he was taken out of the sea."

"Yes, he was. But he was dead before he went in, we think."

"Do you mean he was killed?"

"It's a possibility. I'm sorry."

Lyons sensed that the girl was becoming more composed, so she pressed on with a few questions.

"Teresa, can you give me Terry's mobile phone number?"

Teresa took an iPhone out of her fleece pocket and scrolled through the contacts, turning it around to Lyons when Terry Halpin's photo and details were displayed. Lyons wrote the number into her pocketbook.

"Thanks. Were you in touch with Terry while you were away?"

"No. We made a pact. I'd arranged the trip months ago, and he told me to go off and enjoy myself with the girls and not to worry about him. He said he'd be fine." She dissolved into tears again.

"Do you know any of Terry's friends, Teresa?"

"Just Keith. I don't like him much, but Terry says he's OK. He tried it on with Eleanor once – she's one of the girls I was away with – and when she wasn't having any, he got quite stroppy. He pushed her around a bit and called her terrible names."

"Do you have a number for Keith?"

"Not likely!"

Lyons continued to probe the girl gently for another fifteen minutes, but found that she knew very little of Terry Halpin's activities outside of their relationship. She knew he worked as a sort of builder, and that his family lived in Screebe, but she had never been there, and apart from Keith Gillespie, she knew no other acquaintances of the dead man."

"What kind of vehicle did Terry use, Teresa?" Lyons said.

"He mostly used an old white van. It was a smelly old thing, and it was always full of shit – you know the kind of stuff builders have – old paint tins and bits of wood."

"Did he have any other car at all?"

"Once or twice he turned up in a silver Jeep. He said it was his dad's and he'd borrowed it for the night. That was much better – very comfy."

"OK, Teresa. Well, thanks for your help. If we need to speak to you again, we'll be in touch, and I'm sorry for your loss."

Lyons took the girl's contact details and showed her out.

Chapter Thirteen

When Lyons got back upstairs, Mary Fallon had returned with a bacon, lettuce and tomato sandwich and a cardboard cup of steaming coffee for each of them. She had placed Lyons' change down on the table in the office, and had managed to find two matching plates from the motley collection that the Gardaí kept in their little kitchen.

Before she sat down to tackle her sandwich, Lyons stopped by O'Connor's desk and gave him the number she had got from Teresa.

"John. See what you can find out about that number will you? The phone is probably at the bottom of Galway Bay, but get the records from the company for the last month. Let's see who Terry has been mixing with."

Back in her office, she said, "Thanks, Mary. Dr Dodd is looking for me, but I can't face him on an empty stomach! Let's eat."

When there were just a few crumbs left from the sandwiches, and the coffee was almost gone, Lyons picked up the phone and called the pathologist.

"Dr Dodd. You were looking for me."

"Ah, yes, Inspector. I have a few bits and pieces for you before we get our full report out."

"Great! Shoot."

"Sinéad has been out at Halpin's digs on Eyre Street and recovered a lot of DNA – honestly, the way some people live! We're sending the samples to Dublin to match Halpin's and see about the others. I suspect this Gillespie character's will be amongst them, but with nothing to compare it to, we won't know for sure."

"OK, how long will that take, Doc?"

"I've asked for an expedited analysis, so we should have something tomorrow, late on. Oh, and Detective Sergeant Fahy found a stash of cash at the flat too. Quite a lot, it seems. Sinéad is processing it now."

"Nice. Anything on the body in the van?"

"Well, he was dead for quite a while before the fire. Several days I should think. I'm working on dental records at the moment. That's about all that was left of the poor chap that could give us a clue as to who he is. But it will be slow. God knows how many dentists we'll have to consult – that's if he's from around here at all, so don't hold your breath."

"Is there absolutely no other identification on the body at all, Doctor?" Lyons said.

"About four inches of one leg of his jeans, one sock, and one shoe. The rest was destroyed by the fire. Though he had a wristwatch on. It's in pretty bad shape, but we might be able to coax a serial number off it eventually. That's Sinéad's speciality, as you know."

"What about the van itself? Anything there?"

"You'll have to ask Sinéad about that, Inspector. I'm concentrating on the dead bodies."

"Oh, right. I'll talk to her later. In fact, could you ask her to come over at about five o'clock – we'll be having a briefing then with the day's activity. Thanks for all that. Let me know as soon as you have the DNA analysis, won't you?"

"Yes, of course, will do."

* * *

A few minutes later, Eamon Flynn and Sally Fahy arrived back.

"OK, as we're all here, let's have a quick chat about what we've got so far."

The team drew up a circle in the middle of the open plan. Lyons started by telling them about the visit from Terry Halpin's girlfriend.

"She was pretty cut up. But then she did go off on holiday without him, so I don't know how serious they really were. I should have asked her for a DNA sample to eliminate her from whatever you got from Halpin's flat. I completely forgot. Never mind. We can get it again. What was the McGuire character like?" she said looking at Flynn and Fahy.

Fahy filled her in about her conversation with McGuire, then Lyons said,

"OK. Give the information on the van to John – let's see if it's a match for the burnt-out one at Lough Bollard. Now, we need to prioritize finding this Keith Gillespie. Have we a description or a photograph of him anywhere?"

"I don't think so, boss."

"Right. Well someone ask John to get onto Social Welfare and see if they have any record of him, and maybe even a photograph off his Public Service Card or whatever. Try the driving license people too. They might have a picture. After that, we'll have to start going down through all the Gillespies in the phone book to see if we can locate him, but let's hope it won't come to that. Mary, I want you to go back out to Screebe and spend some time with the Halpins. Hang around, and get them talking. See what you can pick up – oh and confirm that Mr Halpin drives a silver jeep too, will you? Does anyone else think it's funny that there are no mobile phones to be found anywhere around this case?"

"Yes, I thought that too," Eamon Flynn said. "Why don't we get onto the mobile phone operators and see if they can identify a Keith Gillespie. He must be with one of them after all, unless it's an unregistered pay-as-you-go."

"Good idea, Eamon. Anyone else, any ideas?"

"What about a television appeal, boss?" Sally Fahy said.

"Not without a photograph, Sally. TV is a visual medium and we'd look daft if we didn't have a picture for them to broadcast. Let's see what we can dig up first. But that reminds me, has anyone looked into Halpin's bank account?"

No one responded.

"Right. Sally, that's your next job. Mary will find out from his folks where he kept his account, and then we want full records for the last six months, OK?"

"What do want me to do?" Eamon Flynn asked.

"I want you to start looking into this McGuire fella. Go and see him again. Rattle him a bit. If we shake him up, he may let something slip. I'm going to see if I can find the superintendent and bring him up to date."

* * *

Hays was in his office when Lyons knocked on the door.

"Come in, Maureen. How's it going?"

"Have you got a few minutes, Mick?" Lyons said.

Hays looked at his watch and frowned slightly.

"Yeah, just a few though. I have a meeting in about twenty minutes over at the council offices. What's up?"

"Ah, nothing much. I'm supposed to be updating you – but there's nothing to update you with I'm afraid. This thing is a right old mystery. I was hoping you might have some ideas, and anyway I just wanted to see you."

Hays smiled.

"That's nice. Sometimes I think we get too bogged down in our work. Maybe we should snatch a few days away somewhere. What do you think?"

"That could be tricky just now, Mick. I need to make some progress with this case before Plunkett decides to get the big shots in from Dublin. I'd never live that down."

"Hmm... I know what you mean. Look, I really have to go. Would it help if I came to your end-of-day briefing later? I could be down around five-ish if you think that would help at all."

"That would be great. Thanks. We need all the experience and brain power we can muster on this one."

Hays gathered his papers and placed them in a smart burgundy leather portfolio case, and zipped it up. He came out from behind his desk and gripped Lyons gently by the shoulder, and kissed her warmly. She returned his embrace, and broke off after a moment or two.

"Go on, Superintendent, we don't want you late for your meeting, now do we?" she said, smirking and patting him on the behind.

* * *

Sometimes, murder cases can be solved very quickly. Quite often, because of carelessness on behalf of the perpetrator, or where the killing has taken place in a heated moment, it only takes days, or even sometimes hours, to identify the murderer and arrest them. But in cases where the criminal has been operating to a well thought out plan, and where motive is obscure, it can take months or even years to detect the person responsible. In these cases, it is often some totally unrelated or apparently insignificant event that produces new evidence, and the Gardaí have to keep their files open and remain vigilant until the matter can be concluded.

Lyons hoped that this was not one of these cases. When Mick Hays had been an operational officer, they had a reputation for bringing killers to justice in short order. But Lyons couldn't help but feel that this one was different. Nothing about the case stacked up. Not yet at least.

Chapter Fourteen

True to his word, Detective Superintendent Mick Hays arrived into the open plan area at just after five o'clock. Lyons brought the team together, and explained, "I have asked the superintendent to join us this afternoon. He may be able to make some useful suggestions and give us a few pointers," she said, making out that it was her idea so as not to jeopardise her position as SIO.

The team acknowledged Hays, and Flynn got up from his seat, offering it to the senior officer, who declined, and remained standing.

"Let's make a start then. Eamon, did you go and see McGuire?" Lyons said.

"Yes, boss. I see what you mean about him being shifty. He didn't say much, but at least I got a list of a few places where he is having work done at the moment. I'll do a tour of the sites and speak to his workmen – see if any of them knew Halpin well, or might know where Gillespie is hiding."

Just then, Sinéad Loughran came into the office, slightly out of breath.

"Sorry I'm late, Inspector," she said blushing a bit, and looking around for somewhere to sit down quickly. John

O'Connor quickly gave up his seat, and perched on the edge of one of the desks.

"Hi, Sinéad. No problem. We're just getting started. John, any luck with any of the stuff you have been working on?"

"Yes, boss. Firstly, the burnt-out van is nothing to do with McGuire. His van is alive and well and has completely different VIN and reg numbers."

"I see. So, have we any clue on the burnt-out van then?"

"No, sorry. But there's better news about some of the other stuff," O'Connor said.

"I'm glad to hear it. Go on then – don't keep us in suspense!"

"Sorry. Well, Mary found out that Terry Halpin had his bank account with the National Bank in Clifden. I have the details, but as usual, they wouldn't give me any information over the phone, so someone will need to call on them. I did establish that he had just one current account though."

"OK. That's a job for tomorrow. Fancy it, Sally?"

"Yes, fine, boss. I'll let Séan Mulholland know too in case he wants to come along."

"Great. Anything else, John?"

"Yes. Halpin's mobile phone was with Three. Mary found a few bills out at Screebe and I got onto the company to get the records. They were a bit sniffy about it, but they're sending me three months' worth over by email tomorrow. Interestingly, they said that the account was still active."

"What does that mean, John?" Lyons said.

"Apparently, the phone is still making and receiving calls."

"Is it now? Well, you know the drill. Find out what numbers are being called and what numbers are calling it, and most importantly, where the bloody thing is. This could be out first solid lead! Anything on Gillespie?"

"No, sorry, boss. I've got one of the civilian workers ringing all the Gillespies in the 091 area – there are forty-six in the phone book, and I'm getting the unlisted ones from the phone company too. If we don't get a hit with that, I'm going to extend it to 061 and 071. Cast the net a bit wider, so to speak."

"OK, John, that's good work. Any sign of Halpin's laptop anywhere?" Flynn said.

"No, nothing at all, and Mary's been through his room pretty thoroughly now so it's still on the missing list," O'Connor said.

"OK. Thanks. Sinéad, what have you got for us?"

"Quite a bit. Firstly, the van. A few things. There was about eight litres of fuel left in the tank after the fire. Diesel doesn't explode, and the van seems to have burned from the top down and, well, just kind of burnt out before the tyres caught. But the fuel was farm diesel, not road diesel. I'm having it analysed to see if there are any other markers in it that might tell us who supplied it."

"Hmm... interesting. That's not all that unusual though. Quite a lot of people do that to save money. Let us know if you get anything that would tell us where it came from. Anything else?" Lyons said.

"Yes. You know the cash that was found at the bedsit on Eyre Street? I've been examining that closely," Loughran said.

"We always knew you were keen on a few bob, Sinéad," Flynn said, and a ripple of laughter went around the room.

"Ha ha, very funny. But seriously, when I got it under the microscope, I found some plant seeds stuck between the notes, and in the bottom of some of the plastic wrappers. I'll have to get a botanist to have a look at them, but I don't think they're local. There's a Professor Wilson over at the University I can call on. He's helped us out before."

"Cool. Anything else?" Lyons asked.

"Yes, there's more. The van. I found a hidden compartment under the floor. The van has been modified to create a hiding place where the spare wheel usually sits. I understand a few builders do this to keep valuable tools away from opportunist thieves. And it wasn't empty!"

"Jesus, Sinéad, have you ever thought of writing thrillers for a living? Get on with it, will ya!" Lyons said smiling.

"Sorry, yes, well there was an angle grinder, a few cutting disks and an expensive DeWalt battery-operated drill, and perhaps more interesting, some lengths of iron tie bars – you know the ones that are twisted like barley sugar that they use for reinforcing concrete. There were three of them, all about a metre in length."

"Nice one, Sinéad. Have you managed to get any fingerprints off the tools?" Lyons said.

"Yes, I have – a couple of nice clean ones from the DeWalt battery and the plug from the charger. But I haven't had a chance to run them through the database as yet."

Hays, who had been silent up to that point, gave a little cough.

"Yes, Mick, do you want to come in?" Lyons said.

"Thanks," Hays said, and sidestepped up through the group to the front of the room.

"I hope you don't mind me making a suggestion, Inspector, but I wonder if Sinéad could do a comparison between the iron bars found in the van and the little fragment that was taken from Halpin's head wound?"

"Good point. Yes. Sinéad, can you do that first thing tomorrow? We badly need to establish if these two killings are connected, and that would do it. Any sign of blood on any of the bars you found under the van?" Lyons said.

"No. Not from a quick look anyway, but I'll do a more thorough examination in the morning."

"Thanks. Anything else, Superintendent?" Lyons said.

"Just this Gillespie chap. I think you should get onto the airlines and the ferry companies – both here and in the North – and see if there's any sign of a Keith Gillespie travelling. And you need to identify the body in the van. Follow up on the dental records, and go back over Dr Dodd's PM report with a fine-tooth comb. And find out where the cash from Eyre Street comes from. If it's not local, it may help."

"How do you do that, Superintendent?" Loughran asked.

"There's an algorithm that is used with the serial numbers that uniquely identifies the country of origin of the notes. I have a paper on it somewhere on my PC. I'll look it out and send it to you. The chances are they are Irish, but you can never be sure till you have checked."

"Thanks, Mick. Right then. Tasks for tomorrow. Sinéad you'll have your hands full what with the iron bars, the fingerprints, the diesel from the van and the seeds in the money. Sounds like a lot of work. Can you get help?" Lyons said.

"Yeah, no problem. I'll rope in a few willing students. They love this stuff."

"Great. John, will you keep going with the phone companies. Sally, you're going out to Clifden to see the bank manager of the National, and Eamon, you have the various sites that McGuire is working on to visit. Let's meet again this time tomorrow to compare notes, but if anyone has any kind of a breakthrough, let me know at once. OK, thanks, everyone."

The room cleared slowly, and Lyons and Hays retired to her office.

* * *

"Thanks, Mick. I didn't know about the currency thing. Neither did Sinéad. That could be very helpful. Are you ready for home now?"

"No, 'fraid not. I have to write up a report on the meeting earlier at the Council. Yer man wants it before the morning. But it won't take too long. Fancy some grub out somewhere?" Hays said.

"Sounds good. I might just catch Sinéad and go for a glass of wine with her while you're doing your report. Give me a call when you're done and we can go somewhere to eat."

"That's OK then. I'll just slave away over a hot PC while you go boozing with your buddies – see if I care."

Lyons went over to him and put her arms around him.

"Aww, poor diddums. The joys of rank in the Garda Síochána," and she kissed him.

"Right. I best get on. This bloody report won't write itself. I'll call you in a while," Hays said.

Lyons went back out and caught Sinéad Loughran as she was just about to leave. She had been speaking to John O'Connor about the serial numbers of the currency, and they were examining one of the €20 notes that John had removed, trying to figure out the algorithm.

"Hey, Sinéad, fancy a glass of chardonnay?" Lyons said.

"Now why didn't I think of that. Yes please!"

Chapter Fifteen

Maureen Lyons and Sinéad Loughran put on their jackets and went in search of a drink. They wandered into the centre of Galway and ended up in a small, fashionable bistro just off Shop Street where the after work crowd were just beginning to gather.

They managed to grab a table near the back of the place where the bar counter finished, and where they could hear each other comfortably amongst the general hub-bub.

When they both had a large glass of chilled white wine in front of them, they clinked glasses and drank.

"Cheers, Sinéad," Lyons said, enjoying the refreshing acidity of the cold wine.

"So, what's new with you, Maureen? It seems like ages since we had a good old chin wag."

"Ah, ye know, same old same old. Nothing startling to report. But I'm not unhappy, don't get me wrong. It's just... sometimes I wonder what the rest of world is getting up to. What am I missing?"

"God, I'm dead jealous of your set-up, Maureen. A nice home, a stable relationship with a good man, a job that you like – what more could a girl want?" Loughran said.

"I know. I shouldn't complain, and I'm not really. I appreciate all that I have, I really do, but sometimes you just get to thinking that there must be more to life. Anyway, what about you? How's your love life?"

"Non-existent, I'm afraid. Nothing – not a glimmer!"

"That bad, eh? I thought you were getting on OK with that guy, what was his name, Kevin?"

"Long gone, unfortunately. Turns out he wasn't into monogamy. He only made a pass at a friend of mine at a party that I couldn't get to, so I had to jettison him. I'm not having that."

"Are you sure you weren't a bit hasty? After all, it could have been her that started making eyes at him."

"I don't care which of them it was. I'm not putting up with that shit from any bloke, and I doubt if you would either, Maureen."

"No, well you're right there. Thankfully, Mick doesn't seem inclined to stray at all. At least not that I know of, but I think he's straight enough about it."

"See, I told you – you have a good man there. Be careful what you wish for."

"Yeah, I guess you're right. I'm just feeling a bit restless with these two murders to deal with, and no clue as to what's going on – not yet anyway. Have you any ideas?" Lyons said.

"I'd say they are connected, for sure. Wouldn't you agree? It's just too much of a coincidence for them not to be. But you need to track down this Gillespie bloke. He seems to be pivotal to the enquiry, and he can't have just vanished into thin air," Loughran said.

"Yeah, unless he's the body in the van, of course."

"Dodd will have the dental records sorted out in a few days, then we should know if it's him or not. Oh, and did I tell you about the seeds we found in with the packets of money from Eyre Street?"

"No. What about them?"

"Well, they are little brown jobs about two millimetres long, shaped like a rugby ball. I couldn't find anything matching them in our own compendium of flora, so I got authorization to consult a forensic botanist. He's coming on Monday to have a look."

"Cool. Let us know what he says. And maybe your forensic botanist will be hunky – you never know!"

"Give over, will you! I'm not that desperate – yet!"

By this time their glasses were empty, and Lyons, not having heard anything from Hays, called for a refill for both of them. As they were nearly finished their second glass of wine, Lyons' phone started chirping in her handbag. It was Hays.

"Hi. I'm just about done here now. Where are you?"

"Hi, Mick. Just having a drink with Sinéad. Why don't I meet you at the bottom of Shop Street in, say, ten minutes and you can drive. I don't want to have to blow a bag again."

"Yes, fine. See you there. Does Sinéad want to come with us and we could get something to eat somewhere?"

"Hang on, I'll ask her."

Sinéad didn't want to join the other two, so she made her excuses and they parted company.

* * *

The following day was grey and overcast, with an annoying amount of drizzle falling from the leaden sky in the city. It wasn't really raining, but it wasn't dry either. Eamon Flynn donned a raincoat and a rather unflattering baseball cap that he kept in his car, and set off on foot around the narrow streets of Galway. The sites that McGuire had given him were all in the city centre and mostly comprised old cottages in poor condition where elderly folks had lived, unable or not sufficiently interested to keep their places in good repair as their health and wealth declined. McGuire snapped these little houses up at very reasonable prices from the estates of the deceased, the offspring frequently having gone overseas and retaining little interest in their old family home. One of the other sites was an old shop. It had been a haberdashery that had traded in the same place since the 1930s when wool and yarns were frequently purchased for knitting and darning by the women of the town. But knitting and repairing socks had become too time-consuming in the modern era, and eventually the place had to close. McGuire was converting it into yet another fast food outlet. "Just what the city needs – not," Flynn said as he approached the hoarding surrounding the old place.

He visited three sites in all, that morning, and spoke to the workers, many of whom were foreign, mostly from Poland or Romania. This was a common theme in modern-day Ireland. The workers could earn a lot more than they could in their own country, and many of them had sent enough back to their native land to purchase large houses in good locations, while enduring a rather meagre existence in Ireland for a few years to set themselves up.

Although somewhat reluctant to talk to the police, Flynn bought take-away coffees in abundance, and at one site he even rose to a couple of large pizzas as it was coming up to lunch time, and the hot drinks and food relaxed the men who opened up a bit and answered most of his questions.

Halpin and Gillespie were known to the builders at all three sites. The general impression Flynn formed was that they weren't up to much as tradesmen, but were handy enough at heavy work: lugging timber or steel around, helping with the scaffolding where it was needed, and clearing away the inevitable piles of rubbish and rubble that refurbishment entails. But no one had seen either of them for over a week. Flynn pressed the men regarding Gillespie, but still it seemed he hadn't been seen for some time.

* * *

"Ah, come in, girl. Will ya have a cup of tea – I'm just after putting on the kettle?" Séan Mulholland said when Sally Fahy entered the Garda station in Clifden.

"Hello, Séan. Thanks. It's a bad old day for driving out here – there's a lot of mist on the road."

"Nothing new there, Sally. What has you out this way anyway?" Mulholland said, preparing their drinks and opening a new packet of his signature chocolate Goldgrain biscuits.

"I need a word with the manager of the National Bank. It turns out Terry Halpin had his account there, and we need to find out what his financial position was. Do you fancy coming down with me when we've finished this?"

"Ah, no. I'd say you'd do better on your own. He has an eye for a pretty girl has that one. I'd only be in the way."

"Fair enough," Fahy said.

"But I wouldn't say Halpin had much money in the bank, Sally. That family were never very well off, so don't expect to find a big stash."

Fahy continued to chat to Mulholland for another few minutes, and then, having ensured that the man's nose could not be out of joint by her intrusion onto his patch, she headed down the street to the bank.

The manager saw her immediately, and invited her into his office which was a bit dowdy, but spacious, at the back of the public area. When he had heard the nature of Fahy's visit, and made the obligatory comments about what a dreadful tragedy the passing of Terry Halpin was, the manager revealed that Halpin had just €66.37 in his account, and that there had been little movement over the past six months, with just the occasional lodgement of modest amounts and a few ATM withdrawals. Fahy collected a print-out of the account from the man, and left.

* * *

Given the amount of letters after his name when Sinéad Loughran looked up Professor Carl Wilson on the University College Galway's website, she was expecting a man in his fifties or sixties to arrive to assist with the identification of the seeds that had been found in amongst the money recovered from Halpin's bedsit in Eyre Street. How wrong she was.

Wilson was in his thirties. Tall and gangly, with a good mop of curly black hair and a tanned complexion, he carried an Apple MacBook under his arm. Loughran was taken aback by his age, but quickly warmed to the man as she sensed that he was a rather nerdy type and quite obviously an expert of considerable standing in his field.

When pleasantries had been exchanged, Loughran brought Wilson into her lab and showed him the seeds that she had collected in a small round Petri dish on the bench.

"Have you got a tweezers, Sinéad? I need to look at one of these under the microscope."

Loughran handed him the implement, and he gently lifted one of the seeds and placed it on a slide before putting it under the instrument. The image appeared on the screen connected to the device, several times larger than the item itself.

"I don't suppose there were any leaves in with this lot?" Wilson said.

"I think there might have been a few fragments. But they're all dried up and very brittle. Hang on, I'll get them for you."

Loughran produced what just looked like brown dust fragments to the naked eye, and Wilson carefully placed them under the microscope as well. He then opened up his own computer and started tapping away on the keyboard.

After a few minutes, Loughran's curiosity got the better of her, and she said, "Any ideas?"

"Maybe. But I need to check it out a bit further. I'll just take a few photos of this lot and go back and look up some stuff. But if they are what I'm thinking, you're in for a surprise!"

"Aren't you going to give me a clue, Carl?"

"Nope! Not yet anyway. I could be totally wrong."

"Oh, OK. When will you know?"

"Later on. I'll give you a call."

Chapter Sixteen

The detectives met up again in the late afternoon. As usual, Lyons led the meeting, and she started by asking each of them what they had discovered during the day.

"Eamon, – how did you get on visiting McGuire's sites?"

"Not great, boss. I spoke to a good few of his workmen. They all knew Halpin and Gillespie, too, but they hadn't seen either of them for a while. I think they were being fairly straight with me. They're quite cautious not to fall foul of the law in case they get sent home."

"OK. Anything to follow up on?"

"I don't think so, but I think McGuire is quite shifty. He might be worth looking into a bit more."

"Maybe, but we don't have anything to connect him to any of this so far. It wasn't his van that got set on fire, as far as we can tell, and the only very tenuous connection is that Halpin did some work for him. But I agree that it might be worth looking into it a bit more closely – can you get on to that next week, Eamon?"

"Yes, sure."

"Sally, what did you get from the bank in Clifden?"

"Very little, boss. Halpin's bank account was unremarkable and nearly empty. I have the statements back with me in case we want to go over them."

"Not doing very well, are we. Sinéad, can you help us out here by any chance?"

"Of course," she said cheerily. "I had a visit from Carl Wilson from the University. He examined the seeds and some other tiny bits of dead foliage we found in the money and guess what?"

"Stop messing, Sinéad, just tell us!" Lyons said.

Sinéad Loughran consulted her notes.

"They are from a plant called Atriplex Lanfrancoi – I think I'm saying that right – otherwise known as Maltese Cliff Orache, or Bjanka tal-irdum in the vernacular."

"That's easy for you to say. What does it mean?" Flynn said.

"Well, Maltese Cliff Orache is unique to the islands of Malta and Gozo. It apparently grows on a cliff, or on very poor rocky terrain, and this particular variety doesn't grow anywhere else, although there are several other varieties that do."

"And how certain is Professor Wilson about this?" Lyons said.

"I asked him that. He's said ninety to ninety-five percent certainty, and he said he could germinate a couple of the seeds to be one hundred percent sure if we wanted him to."

"I see. So Halpin and, or, Gillespie had a pile of cash that appears to have come from Malta – is that it?" Lyons said.

"Looks like it, yeah. A bit odd though, isn't it?" Loughran said.

Lyons could see that John O'Connor was itching to get in on the conversation.

"Yes, John, what is it?" Lyons said.

"That's not all, boss. The money we found in the bedsit in Eyre Street was issued in Malta too – all of it. I used the thing Superintendent Hays sent down to check the serial numbers. There's no doubt – it's Maltese money."

"Hmm... there can't be any doubt then. What is Malta noted for these days apart from sunny holidays?"

"Money laundering, it seems. There was a TV programme on it a few weeks back on the BBC. Seems the Eastern Europeans, or more likely the Russians have got their sticky fingers all over it," Flynn said.

"Yeah, but two lads from Galway are hardly likely to be involved in that sort of thing, surely? This thing is doing my head in. Let's leave it for the weekend and come back to it with clear heads on Monday morning. Thanks everyone. Have a good one."

When the team broke up, Sinéad Loughran followed Lyons into her office.

"Fancy a drink, Maureen?"

"No, not tonight, Sinéad. I want to get home. I have mountains of ironing to get through and I don't want it hanging over me all weekend. Some other time – unless there's something specific you need to chat about?"

"No. It'll keep. I'd hate to distract you from your domestic duties! Do you have to iron Mick's shirts?" she said with a smirk.

"No, I bloody don't! Just the sheets and pillowcases and my own stuff. He does his own shirts, and anything else he needs ironing. Unless he's under a lot of pressure, then I might give him a hand. He does the same for me."

"God! You're gas. Who would have thought!"

"I know what you mean. It's bonkers – but somehow it works. How was the lovely professor, by the way?"

"Nerdy. I doubt if I had been standing there naked he'd have even noticed me to be honest. He's more interested in flora than fauna."

"You should try that next time – see if it works! But did you fancy him. C'mon, spill!"

"Dunno. Too much like hard work finding out if you ask me," Loughran said.

"You're hopeless, Sinéad. You're going to end up an old spinster if you don't stop being so picky. Anyway, I'd better get going. See you next week," Lyons said, putting on her jacket and fishing in her handbag for her car keys.

"Yeah. See ya."

Chapter Seventeen

Hays awoke at half past nine on Sunday morning. It was a lovely day, and the view from their bedroom out over the sea at Salthill was spectacular, the sun making the surface of the calm water look like solid silver. Lyons was still asleep, so Hays hopped out of bed, put on his dressing gown and slippers, and went downstairs to the kitchen. Fifteen minutes later he was back, carrying a tray laden with two glasses of orange juice, two plates of scrambled egg on toast and a jug of hot coffee.

"Aw, God, you're an angel, Mick. Thanks a lot," Lyons said, sitting up in the bed and wiping the sleep from her eyes. The two of them tucked into the breakfast with some enthusiasm.

"Hey, I forgot to tell you," Lyons said between mouthfuls, "I had a call from the guy that owns the flat I used to live in down by the river in town."

"You mean the one that you still hold the lease on and dodgily sub-let to that handsome young Garda with the Honda Pan European motorbike?"

"The very one. That reminds me, he promised me a go on the back of that thing. I must remind him next time I'm collecting the rent. Anyway, the old guy is retiring and he wants to sell up – the whole place, both flats – and he's offered me first refusal. What do you think?"

"Wow! See, I knew you were going to become a woman of property eventually," Hays said.

Lyons punched him gently in the stomach.

"Feck off, Hays. No seriously, do you think I should have a go at it?"

"I know the top flat is in pretty good shape. What's the ground floor one like?"

"I haven't been in it for ages. It probably just needs a lick of paint. And it would let really easily."

"Has the old guy said how much he wants for the place?"

"He said he'll take a hundred and twenty grand, and if I was interested he'd be in no hurry. He'd give me time to get the finances organised. Don't suppose you'd fancy coming in on it with me?" she said, tentatively, looking carefully at his expression to judge his instant reaction.

"Hmm... might do. Fifty-fifty?"

"Well, sixty-sixty actually, but yeah, halvos."

"And I suppose you just happen to have sixty grand tucked away in your knicker drawer, Inspector!"

"Well, not quite. But I wouldn't have to borrow too much. Tell you what. What are you up to today?"

"I was thinking of asking Peadar out in the boat. It's a lovely day, and I kinda owe him one after that incident with Halpin. Would you be OK with that?"

"Yes, of course. I might nip out to Athenry to see Sheila. Would you mind if I ran the property thing past her?"

Sheila was Lyons' sister who lived on what had been the family farm near Athenry. Although it had been left between them, Lyons had had no interest in farming, and the girls came to an arrangement whereby Lyons retained a financial interest in the place, while Sheila and her husband ran the operation. It was a good set-up, and had worked well for all concerned.

"No, 'course not. She has a good head on her. She'd be able to advise you, but it sounds like a runner. Do you think we'd be able to beat the old guy down a bit. A hundred grand is a much rounder figure."

"I wouldn't like to do that, Mick. A hundred and twenty is a good price as it is, and fair's fair."

"Yeah, you're right. I'm spending too much time trying to whittle down budgets and expenditure for the Gardaí. It must have got to me."

"So, you're happy with one-twenty then?" she said.

"Yeah. You're right – it's a fair price. A hundred and twenty it is."

"Great. I'll catch you later then," she said getting out of bed and heading for the shower.

* * *

Mary Fallon was also awoken that Sunday by the bright sunlight streaming in through her bedroom window. She had a place in Clifden where she thought she was going to be stationed when she had completed her training, but Séan Mulholland had decided that her talents would be more useful in Roundstone, so he had sent her there to assist Pascal Brosnan, doubling the strength of the force in the little town. Mary didn't like to break the arrangement she had with her landlady, so she stayed on in Clifden, and if truth were told, she quite enjoyed the fact that she wasn't living on top of her work, and she looked forward to the daily drive out along the old bog road by the sea between her flat and Roundstone village. Maybe next year, if she stayed on in Roundstone, she'd see about moving, but for now Clifden suited her just fine.

When she had showered and had her modest breakfast of cereal and strong coffee, she sat lingering at the table and her thoughts turned to the case they had been investigating. She had no plans for the day, so she had an idea. She called her colleague.

"Hi, Pascal. Hope I didn't disturb your beauty sleep!"

"Ah, you're grand, Mary. What can I do for you?" Brosnan said. He had been up a good while at this stage and was thinking about starting redecoration of the spare bedroom in the smart little bungalow that he owned a few hundred metres from the Garda station. The room wasn't in a bad state, but he liked things fresh and clean, so he had decided to give it the once over.

"Are you busy, Pascal?" Mary said.

"Not yet. But I could be. What have you in mind?" he said, wondering where this was leading. Mary was very attractive, and he did fancy her, but he was very reluctant to do anything about it, knowing that if they became romantically involved, it could lead to all sorts of difficult complications.

"I've been thinking about this Terry Halpin thing. You wouldn't care for a trip out to that pub in Kilnatrá, would you? We could grab some lunch. I just have a hunch that the place has more to tell."

"Hmm... OK. But do you think we ought to inform Mulholland or the gang back in Galway what we're up to?"

"Let's see if we find anything first. There's no point bothering them on a Sunday. I'll come in. See you in an hour or so."

When the call was ended, Pascal Brosnan felt a bit uneasy about Mary's proposal for what was to all intents and purposes an unauthorized operation. They had no license to indulge in such a thing, and he knew Mulholland in particular would be unhappy with this type of deviation from protocol. But he liked Mary, and spending a few hours in her company was a lot more enticing than rolling emulsion paint, so he relaxed, and went to change into his best casual clothes.

* * *

They took Mary Fallon's Ford Fiesta and set off through Roundstone and on round the winding coast road toward Carna. If anything, the day had improved since early morning, and the pale blue sky, peppered with small white cotton-wool clouds contrasted beautifully with the rugged heathland to make a picture postcard vista as they drove along. The roads were narrow, bordered by dry stone walls, and occasionally Mary had to pull in to let another vehicle pass, but she was in no hurry, and as they met the few cars going in the other direction, she saluted politely, as was the custom on these quiet country lanes.

They arrived at Kilnatrá at twenty to one. The car park of Tigh Oisrí had about a dozen cars scattered around, and Mary pulled in at the end of a row of four so that there was clear sight of the building from the car. Pascal was about to get out, when Mary said, "Hold on a sec, Pascal," and she nodded towards the side of the pub. There was a large set of wooden gates at the entrance to a yard, and inside the gates a blue Ford Transit van was stopped with its rear doors open, facing them. A man in dirty jeans and an equally scruffy polo shirt was loading boxes from the van into the side door of the building. As he came back out each time, he glanced furtively at the car park. On his third trip, he seemed to be taking quite an interest in the couple in Mary's Fiesta.

Suddenly, Mary leaned over, put her arms around Pascal's neck and drew him close, as if in an embrace.

"He's spotted us. Just pretend we're a couple and make it look natural. Have you seen the registration number on the van?" she whispered in his ear.

Pascal, taking his colleague's lead, put his arms around her shoulder, and said, "Yes, I spotted that. And there's kegs inside the van too. Can you memorize the number plate?"

"I have. That's an Antrim plate if I'm not mistaken. Interesting," Fallon said.

"What happens now," Brosnan said, feeling a little uncomfortable with the situation.

"We get out and go for a walk. You'll have to hold my hand – make it look like we're a couple," she said with a twinkle in her eye.

"Oh, right."

They got out of the car and walked away from the pub towards the coastline. There was a very gentle breeze blowing in from the west, and the sea itself was a shimmering aquamarine colour, with the waves just gently lapping at the rocky shore.

"Looks like McDermott is stocking up with smuggled booze from Northern Ireland. That guy with the van looked right dodgy," Mary said as they strolled along. Brosnan was still holding her hand.

"Ah, I suppose it's difficult enough to make ends meet out here in the sticks. And it's a short season too, so I 'spose he has to do what he can with what he's got," Brosnan said.

"Yeah, but still and all, that's not right. Do you think we should report him to the Revenue?"

"Maybe. I'll talk to Séan about it next week and see if he wants to do anything. But I'd say he'll just want to warn him off. We'll see."

"Sorry, I'm new to all this. I guess there are different ways of dealing with this sort of thing."

"There are. And Mulholland usually gets it right. He's no eejit."

They walked around in a large circle, bringing them back to the rear of Tigh Oisrí where there were tables and chairs set out in the glorious sunshine. As they sat down at one of the tables near the entrance, they heard the Transit van taking off, going a good deal quicker than they would have expected for the nature of the roads.

Cathal McDermott came and served them their lunch – they opted for the seafood platter for two, and it didn't disappoint. McDermott wasn't sure if he recognised Mary from previously, but he said nothing in any case, as he busied himself with the thirty or so patrons.

Mary paid the bill amid much protestation from her colleague.

"Stop it now, Pascal. This was my idea, so my treat. You can return the favour at some stage," she said, putting two crisp twenty euro notes down on the counter inside the pub.

The girl behind the bar took the money and went off to the till to ring it up and get Mary her change. When she came back, Mary said to her, "I don't suppose you've seen Keith Gillespie around recently at all? He was supposed to be doing some work for me last week, but he never turned up."

"Is that the fella that worked with the poor lad that was drowned?" the girl said.

"Yes, I believe so, Terry Halpin, wasn't it?" Mary said, trying to be as nonchalant as possible.

"I think that Keith fella was in here yesterday. Yes, he was, He was with Hugh Halpin. The two of them had a meal and a few pints. I'm sure it was him. Scruffy-looking lad, but nice enough."

Brosnan decided to intervene before Mary blew their cover.

"That's grand, so. Sure, he must be round and about. We'll catch him tomorrow or the next day. Thanks very much." He took Mary by the arm and led her back out to the car park.

"Sorry about that, Mary, but I was afraid you were beginning to sound like a policewoman!"

"No, you're grand. Like I say, I'm new to all this. But it's interesting all the same, isn't it? Do you think we should inform Inspector Lyons?"

"We'll do it the proper way, Mary. Tomorrow, you can call Séan Mulholland and tell him what you found out. He'll inform Lyons, for sure, but we can't go over his head. He'd be rightly pissed off if that happened. And don't say anything about the van with the smuggled booze. I'll raise that with him later in the week."

"OK. You're right. You're fond of the sergeant, aren't you, Pascal?"

"He's been very good to me, Mary. I know he has his own way of doing things, and he doesn't always follow the manual, but he's a damn fine cop and a decent man as well. When you hear some of the stories about what others have to put up with from these old timers, you don't know how lucky we are to have Mulholland."

"I guess. But he's not great with women in the force, is he?"

"He's from another era, Mary. It's understandable. But he has a great deal of admiration for Maureen Lyons. You know, they both used to be sergeants at the same time before Lyons got her promotion. And I can tell you, the respect is mutual too. She thinks a lot of him."

"Ah, that explains it. I was wondering why they were on first name terms. I suppose I'll have to call you 'sir' or 'boss' when you get your stripes!" she said, nudging him in the tummy with her elbow.

"You can start now, if you like."

"Feck off, Brosnan!"

But they were holding hands again.

* * *

Later that evening, Hays and Lyons were together at home. Hays had prepared a substantial meal for them both, and opened a bottle of Lyons' favourite red wine to go with it. When she got back from her sister's, she was mightily impressed.

"Well, aren't you the domestic goddess, then, Mick Hays?" she said, smiling broadly and planting a soft kiss on his willing lips.

"Ah, just something I rustled up, but I'm warning you, I'm starving. Nothing like a few hours on the water to build an appetite."

"How did it go with Peadar?" she said, removing her jacket and placing it over the back of the kitchen chair.

"Grand. He's a really nice guy, and a good sailor too – hardly surprising I guess, given his involvement with the lifeboat."

Hays was serving up the meal that he had prepared, and Lyons had to admit that it both looked and smelled delicious.

"What about you? How's Sheila and the gang?" he asked.

"Great! And you'll never guess what."

"You're right, I never will."

"She only said she could liberate a few grand from the farm to give me towards the place in Galway. I said not to – that they might need it for some improvements or some new equipment – but she said no, they had had a good couple of years and there was quite a surplus. She'd have to talk to Séamus about it, but she said I deserved it, and it was rightfully mine in any case."

"Was she talking a loan?"

"No. She mentioned a dividend or something. I don't know how it works, but it wouldn't be a loan."

"That's terrific. Will you go for it?"

"I'm not sure. I'll give it some serious thought though. It would make things a lot easier. By the way this is scrumptious, Mr Chef," she said, raising her glass in salute to Hays' culinary achievements.

Chapter Eighteen

By nine o'clock Monday morning the murder meeting was in full swing. Lyons was leading, and the rest of the Galway team were sitting around the open plan, where Sinéad Loughran had joined them.

"Right, everyone. There's been a few developments over the weekend you should all know about. I had a call a few minutes ago from Séan Mulholland. He told me that Pascal Brosnan and Mary Fallon were out at Kilnatrá yesterday for lunch, and they got talking to the barmaid. It seems Keith Gillespie was in the place on Saturday in the company of Hugh Halpin – Terry Halpin's father. So we need to get out to Screebe pronto and find out what's going on. Sally, I want you with me as soon as we've finished here. Eamon, get everything you can on McGuire. Finances, planning permissions, employees, previous history – anything and everything you can dig up. Get John to give you a hand."

"Right, will do," Eamon Flynn said.

"Inspector, there's something else," Sinéad Loughran said.

"Yes, Sinéad, what is it?"

"I came in Saturday morning and did some more work on the clothes from the guy we found in the van. One of his shoes was more or less untouched – a sort of trainer, or loafer. It had a Spanish manufacturer's name on the insole, so I checked it out. It had the brand name Paco Fernandes inside, so I looked up that manufacturer on the web. Their website is very informative, and there's a 'Where to Buy' button that lists all their stockists. They sell through outlets all over Spain and the Spanish Islands, and even have one or two places in Italy carrying their shoes. But most interesting of all is that they have a retailer in Valletta, Malta that sells them. I took a note of the shop name and phone number."

"So, all roads lead to Malta then. That's good work, Sinéad, thanks. Let's park that for the moment till we get a handle on this Gillespie chap. I want him downstairs, preferably today, answering questions."

John O'Connor raised his hand.

"I could follow up the shoe thing, Inspector, if you like. Everyone in Malta speaks English. If I could get details of the shoe from Sinéad, I could ring the shop and see if they have any records that could be useful."

"Good one, John. Yes, do that for us, but prioritize Eamon's work first please. Now, before we all go off in different directions, do we have the reg number of the burnt-out van?" Lyons said.

Sinéad Loughran spoke up. "Yes, I have it here. It was a Northern Ireland plate – here we are – 56319 JDZ. I have the VIN number too if we need it."

"OK, Sinéad, can you get someone to follow that up for us? Find out who the registered keeper for that number is and so on, see if it's been spotted anywhere, you know the drill."

"Sure, will do."

"Right. We'll meet again at five for an update. Let's get busy – chop chop!" Lyons said.

* * *

Lyons and Fahy could have taken the coast road out to Screebe, passing Barna, Inverin and Costelloe, but that route could be slow, so Lyons opted for the N59 that took them through Moycullen, Oughterard and on to Maam Cross, where they turned left onto the R336, locally known as the Furnace Road, because of the old peat-burning electricity generating station that was located at Screebe, abandoned finally in 1989. The station produced 5MW of electricity, but more importantly, employed quite a large number of subsistence farmers, allowing them to supplement their meagre income and provide an outlet for the turf that was cut from the bog.

It was a typical Connemara day, with heavy grey clouds overhead promising rain for later on, when the two detectives pulled up outside the Halpin household. Hugh Halpin's silver jeep was parked outside in a sort of layby that had been created in the grass to allow traffic to pass freely when he was at home.

Lyons and Fahy went to the front door, and finding it open, knocked on the frame. They could see Mrs Halpin inside working away at the kitchen table, baking. The woman wiped her hands in her floral apron, and shuffled towards the door.

"Good morning, Mrs Halpin. Is your husband around?" Lyons asked.

"Oh yes, eh... sorry, I've forgotten your name. Yes, Hugh is out the back in the shed. Do you want me to call him for you?"

"It's Lyons. Inspector Lyons, and this is my colleague Detective Sergeant Sally Fahy. Yes please. May we come in?"

"Oh, yes, of course. Sorry. Come in and sit down. Excuse the mess. I'm not myself today," the woman said, turning away and heading for the back door that led out into a large yard to the rear of the little cottage.

A minute or two later, the Halpins came back into the kitchen. Hugh Halpin looked puzzled, and went to the sink to wash his hands. When he had finished, he turned to the two detectives. "Well, ladies, what can we do for you today?"

Hugh Halpin sat down, so Lyons and Fahy sat too, making sure to keep their clothes away from the flour that was spread out on the table.

"Can I offer you a cup of tea?" Mrs Halpin said.

"Thanks, that would be lovely," Fahy said, getting in before Lyons could decline the woman's gesture. She was parched.

"Mr Halpin, can I ask if you have seen Keith Gillespie recently?" Lyons said, keen to make progress.

Halpin looked at her but said nothing.

"Mr Halpin?" Lyons prompted.

"I suppose you already know, otherwise you wouldn't be here, would you?" he said.

"Why don't you tell us about it?" Lyons said.

"He called me the other day. He asked to meet me, so I suggested the pub down at Kilnatrá. We met there on Friday for a while. That's all."

"What did he want?"

"He wanted to talk about Terry. He was keen to explain that he had nothing to do with his death."

"I see. Did he have any explanation for why he is lying low?" Fahy asked.

"He said that he was afraid that the Gardaí would assume that he was involved in some way, and would give him a hard time."

"How did he contact you?" Lyons said.

"He called my mobile. I got quite a shock, because it came up as 'Terry' on my phone. But he explained that he is using his phone now."

"I see. When he said he had nothing to do with your son's death, did you believe him?" Fahy said.

"I don't have much choice, do I?"

"It would have been helpful if you had let us know when he contacted you. As you know, we are anxious to talk to Keith, Mr Halpin," Lyons said.

"He asked me not to."

"All the same, we do need to talk to him. Did he suggest you should contact him again, or meet him?"

"No. But you can call him on Terry's phone."

"Did he say where he was staying?" Fahy said.

"No, he didn't. But he looked a bit rough. I'd say he's camping out somewhere."

"Did he ask you for money?"

Halpin looked down at his boots, and said nothing.

"Mr Halpin?" Lyons prompted again.

"Yes, he did. I gave him €50."

"Look, we need your full co-operation if we are to have any chance of bringing the person or persons responsible for the death of your son to justice, Mr Halpin. We need to know everything that's going on around this tragic case. Can you reassure me that you will contact us if there are any other developments – no matter how insignificant you may feel they are?" Lyons said.

Hugh Halpin said nothing, but Mrs Halpin spoke up. "Of course we will. We're just as anxious as you are to get justice for Terry, aren't we, Hugh?"

"Yes, yes of course," the man said.

A silence fell upon the little group, and Lyons and Fahy drank their tea. There was little more to be said. Fahy checked with Mrs Halpin that they had a correct record of Terry Halpin's mobile phone number, and confirmed that Terry had been a subscriber to the Three network. Lyons put the number into her own mobile phone. After a respectable interval, they got up and said goodbye to the couple.

Outside in the car, Lyons said to Fahy, "What do you make of that then?"

"Bloody weird if you ask me. And I don't think Halpin was telling the whole story, do you?"

"No, I don't. Still, we have to be careful not to be seen to be harassing bereaved parents. But I'm not happy about him at all. Let's see if we can get hold of Gillespie and find out what really happened in the pub," Lyons said.

Chapter Nineteen

Back at the station Lyons asked John O'Connor to set up a recording of the phone call she was going to make to Keith Gillespie. She also asked him to get onto Three and put them on standby to trace the call to the nearest mast while she was speaking to him.

When all that was arranged, she brought Fahy into her office and dialled the number from the landline on her desk.

Halpin's phone, now in the care of Keith Gillespie, rang six times before it was answered by voicemail.

"It's Terry. Leave a message," was all that it said, and then the customary beep sounded and Lyons spoke.

"Keith, this is the Gardaí from Galway. We need to speak to you. Please call back or come into the Garda Station at Mill Street in Galway when you get this message. My name is Inspector Lyons." She reeled off her own mobile number knowing that the caller ID on the station's phone would not have appeared on the mobile at the far end of the call.

Lyons hung up and looked at Fahy, who just shrugged.

John O'Connor put his head round the door.

"Nothing, boss. They couldn't track it precisely, but they did say that it was out west somewhere, if that's any good."

"Not a lot, John, but thanks anyway."

The two women were sitting there not quite sure what to do next when Lyons' mobile phone started ringing in her pocket. She looked at the screen before answering, and was surprised to see that it spelled out Terry Halpin.

"Hello, Keith, thanks for ringing back. This is Inspector Lyons."

"It wasn't me, I didn't harm Terry. I wouldn't – I swear," the man on the other end of the line said. He sounded like he had a bad cold, and was heavily congested.

"Look, Keith, we need to speak to you properly. Now I promise you have nothing to worry about if what you say is true, but we need to talk to you. Can you come into the station here?"

"Not bleeding likely!" Gillespie said. "If you lot get me in there you'll fit me up. I'll never get out."

Lyons looked at Fahy who was listening to both sides of the conversation intently.

The call went silent for a moment while Lyons thought what best to do.

"OK, well, would you be willing to meet me on my own? No tricks. You say when and where, and I'll come by myself. It's the only chance you have to clear your name, Keith."

Gillespie thought about this for what seemed like a long time.

"Maybe. Promise you won't try and grab me or bring loads of backup," he said nervously.

"I promise. Just you and me. Now where and when do you suggest?"

"Better to get it over with," he said, and was seized by a fit of coughing. When he had recovered, he went on, "I'll be at an old derelict cottage out in Ballyconneely – you know the one where that fella that killed the foreign girl used to live. It's in ruins, but I'll be able to see you coming from a long way off, so if there's anyone with you, I'll be away and you'll never find me. OK?"

"OK, yes I know the place" – as if Lyons could ever forget it – "when?"

"Tomorrow at half ten in the morning. And leave your car at the top of the track and walk down, and no funny business."

"Right. I'll see you tomorrow morning then, and you have my word, there will be no funny business as you call it."

The line went dead.

"Jesus, boss! Are you sure about this? You'll be a sitting duck," Fahy said.

"Eh, not quite, Sally. I have a plan!"

* * *

The following morning was bright and sunny with just a few patchy clouds scurrying across the sky.

At ten past ten, Mary Fallon and Pascal Brosnan, dressed in civilian clothes, pulled Mary's little Ford Fiesta into the viewing point by the bridge in Ballyconneely. They stayed in the car, just as any normal couple would do, admiring the view out across the narrow strip of bog, across the golden beach and out to the Atlantic Ocean. Then Brosnan got out and pretended to take photographs with his phone. As he surveyed the scene, and focused briefly on the old cottage where Gillespie had determined he was to meet Lyons, he could see nothing out of place, nor any sign of a presence.

Garda Jim Dolan, one of Sergeant Séan Mulholland's men, had managed to find an ill-fitting old grey two-piece suit and a collarless striped shirt which he wore uncomfortably under an old greasy peaked cap as he meandered across the fields nearby, accompanied by a borrowed black and white sheep dog who couldn't quite figure out what was happening, but was nevertheless enjoying being outdoors with his temporary master. Dolan had Wellington boots on his feet that squelched in the soggy ground, and slowed his progress, and a stout hawthorn stick which was typical in these parts. But he was alert all the same, and assumed that he looked like any of the rugged farmers that kept a few sheep out on the rough heathland to supplement their pension.

Lyons arrived at the old overgrown track that led to the broken-down cottage at just after twenty-five past ten. She drove her Volvo down the rutted lane, with an occasional rock bottoming on the underside of the car as it bounced over the uneven ground. She stopped at the place where the track divided, and got out, being careful to lock the vehicle, and place the key deep into her trouser pocket.

Lyons walked on to the yard in front of the old homestead, her mind being taken back to when Mary Maguire had lived there in apparent harmony with her husband, unaware of his philandering, and eventually murderous ways.

As she approached the front of the building, she could see that the largely rotten front door was ajar. She called out, "Keith. Keith, are you in there?"

There was no reply, so she gingerly approached the entrance and peeked inside. The kitchen of the old place was bright, with the sun streaming in through the roof, much of which had been ripped off the house by the Atlantic gales. In the centre of the room, the old wooden kitchen table was still in place, now gone green with moss, and seated on a chair at the far side of it was a dishevelled-looking young man with a wild shock of fair hair, huddling in a stained brown overcoat.

"Keith?" she said, as she ventured further into the room.

"Aye. Come in, Inspector. Are you on your own now, no messing?"

"Yes, but there is something I need to tell you before we start talking. I have to send a text message with a code every fifteen minutes to indicate that I am OK. If it's not received, Gardaí from Clifden will come out in force."

"Fair enough. Leave your phone here on the table then."

Lyons took one of the two mobile phones she was carrying out of her jacket pocket and placed it on the table in plain sight. She then drew up another of the chairs that had somehow survived the ravages of the weather and was more or less in working order, and took a seat.

"So, Keith, what's the story?"

Chapter Twenty

Eamon Flynn was restless. He had spent a good two hours staring into his PC trying to find out anything and everything about Senan McGuire. He had searched all the usual websites such as Facebook, Instagram and LinkedIn, but had managed to find only the flimsiest details about the man from Derry who plied his trade as a builder of sorts in Galway.

"I've had enough of this," Flynn said to no one in particular.

He logged off his computer, put on his jacket and left the station on foot. A few minutes later he found himself in Dominick Street at the door of McGuire Enterprises. He went through the usual ritual to gain access, but this time, when he climbed the stairs, he was greeted by the man himself.

"Good morning, officer. How can we help you today?" McGuire said.

Flynn nodded towards the private office, and McGuire, taking the hint, led the way.

When they were both seated, McGuire offered Flynn coffee which he declined. McGuire sensed that Flynn was in a very business-like mood, and he wasn't wrong.

"So, what's on your mind?" McGuire said.

"Can you tell me a little about your business, Mr McGuire?" he began.

"What's there to tell? I'm a builder. I buy up a few properties that need attention, fix them up and then either flip them on, or rent them out. It's not complicated."

"And how many of these properties would you have on the go at any time?" Flynn said, not quite sure where this line of questioning was taking him.

"It depends. Right now, I have the shop on Market Street, the place on Eyre Street and three other fixer-uppers in various parts of the city."

"And how come you're operating this business in Galway? Aren't there enough broken down properties in Derry to keep you busy?"

"There are, for sure, but you see I'm married to a Galway girl, and she's very persuasive. So here we are," McGuire said, holding out his hands palm side up in the time honoured gesture.

"How long had Terry Halpin worked for you?"

"It was an on and off sort of thing. I gave him work when he asked – he was a good worker. But he seemed to have other fish to fry as well, so it wasn't constant. You've met most of my workforce, Inspector. As you have seen they are nearly all casual. Halpin was just another one of those."

"And that was the extent of your relationship with the man, is that right?"

"Well, I wouldn't call it a relationship, but yes, he just worked for me from time to time."

"Mr McGuire, we believe Terry Halpin was killed approximately two and a half weeks ago. He was murdered, and then dumped in the sea where his body was recovered some time afterwards. Can you account for your movements around that time?"

"Surely you don't think I had anything to do with it, Inspector?"

"As I was saying, can you account for your movements?"

"I'm not sure. I was here in Galway, just doing the normal things. Visiting the sites where the work is going on. Spending time in the office doing the paperwork and making arrangements for various contracts, and apart from that I was home with my wife. But I can't give you an hour by hour breakdown, I'm afraid. Can you remember exactly where you were every moment that long ago?"

"Do you ever visit the pub out at Kilnatrá?" Flynn asked.

"I've been there once or twice, but it's been a while."

"How long ago?"

"Some months, as far as I can remember, why?"

"So we won't find your vehicle on the CCTV footage from around the time that Terry Halpin went into the drink then?"

"Look, Inspector, I'm not happy with this line of questioning. I've told you as much as I can. Now, I'd like to be able to help you further, but I'm afraid I have nothing more to add, and I'm quite busy today."

Flynn didn't budge. He just looked intently into McGuire's eyes and said nothing. Moments passed, and the two men just stared at each other. Then Flynn broke the silence.

"What is your connection with Malta, Mr McGuire?"

The question took McGuire by surprise. His eyes flared and he quickly looked away, and he thought for a few seconds before answering.

"My brother Ardal lives there – why do you ask?"

"Do you visit him often?"

"A few times a year. I have a place there too. Just a small town-house in a little complex out by St Paul's Bay. It's very peaceful, and we enjoy it."

"How long have you owned that?"

"About six years now. But listen, Inspector, what relevance can any of this have to the unfortunate death of

Mr Halpin? I really don't see how I can be of any further help."

"What does your brother do for a living?"

"He's in import-export of some kind. I really don't know the details."

"And do you have any business dealings with him at all?"

"No, of course not. What would I be doing involved in that sort of thing. I have my own business which I'd very much like to be getting on with if you don't mind!"

Flynn sensed that he had overstayed his welcome by quite some measure, and feeling that he was unlikely to get anything else useful from the builder, he got up and left. On the way back to the station though, his mind was working overtime.

Back at his desk, he logged back into his PC, and armed with the new information, did a deep search for Ardal McGuire in Malta, but strangely found nothing. Nothing at all. There was no website associated with the man, no entries for him on Facebook or any other social media platform, and even searching 'Malta, import-export companies' revealed nothing that could be connected to McGuire. There were only a few of these companies listed in the Maltese Business Directory, and when he went looking, they all displayed a list of the main contacts, but Ardal McGuire was not among any of them.

Next, Flynn brought up a map of St Paul's Bay in Malta. The area was quite extensive, if you included Bugibba, which was on the sea side of the region, and was densely populated with all kinds of buildings, including hotels, apartment blocks and tourist attractions. But Flynn could find no obvious link to what McGuire had told him, although he did see that there was a complex known as The Shamrock Apartments, and he wondered for a moment if that's where Ardal McGuire had his home.

Flynn sat back and thought for a few minutes. There was nothing for it – he'd have to go and see

Superintendent Mick Hays – but he felt that he should wait for Lyons to return before making the trip upstairs.

Chapter Twenty-one

"So, Keith. Tell me about you and Terry Halpin. How did you meet?" Lyons asked.

"We were on a training course together. You know, one of them ones that's supposed to set you up in a job for life. Bloody useless, if you ask me. But the money was OK, and I suppose I did learn a bit about the building trade."

"Was this in Galway?"

"Yeah. It was out on the Mervue. That place with the funny name."

"And you hit it off with Terry, I presume?"

"Not at first. But as the course went on we kinda did, and then we got a few jobs together doing a bit of work. The teacher organised it. I reckon he was getting a cut, 'cos the money was shite."

"What happened then?"

"When the course was over, we was introduced to this McGuire character, and he said he could give us work cash in hand like. He had several places in the city that needed doing up."

"Where were you and Terry living at this stage?"

"Terry was at home with his folks, and I was dossing anywhere around."

"And when did you get the place together in Eyre Street?"

"A few months back. McGuire said we could use it till the place was fixed up. It was handy enough, if not exactly luxurious."

Lyons picked up the mobile phone from the table and keyed in a short text message, sent it, and replaced the phone on the table.

"Keith, when we searched the flat, we found some money hidden in a backpack. Quite a bit of money. Where did that come from?"

"See, I'm telling you, I don't know. I was never involved with Terry's other business. I just did me work and got me pay and had a few beers at the weekend. But he was into other shit. I didn't want to get involved."

"But you are involved, Keith. You must have known what he was up to. Where his extra cash was coming from," Lyons said.

"I'm telling ya, I didn't know shit. I didn't want to know. He was up to something with that McGuire bloke. He's right shifty, he is. And every now and then he'd go off for a day or two on his own and when he came back he'd have some readies that he'd stash in the bedsit. That's all I know – I swear."

"Did either of you ever drive a van for McGuire?"

"I don't have a license. I don't know about Terry, but I don't think he drove a van. I would have seen it parked outside or something. Why?"

"It's just a line of inquiry we are following. So, what do you think McGuire is up to – apart from refurbishing property?"

"Search me. I wouldn't put anything past him," Gillespie said.

"Are you seriously telling me, Keith, that you lived with Terry, you worked together, and yet you still don't know what he was getting up to?"

"See, I said you wouldn't believe me. That's why I didn't want to come in. You're trying to fit me up for his murder, and it had nothing to do with me, I swear."

Gillespie was becoming agitated, and it looked to Lyons as if he might be preparing to make a run for it. She hoped that Dolan and the two Gardaí from Roundstone were being vigilant.

"OK, take it easy, Keith. No one is accusing you of anything. We're just trying to find out what happened to Terry. And I'm sure you've heard that there was another body found in a burnt-out van as well. Do you know anything about that?"

"No, I bloody don't! I'm telling ya – I'm just a humble jobbing builder. I've nothing to do with any of this."

Lyons didn't say anything for a few moments. She was sizing up Keith Gillespie, wondering just how far she could push him before he decided to bolt. She didn't want that. Gillespie was fidgeting, and was obviously very uneasy, but still, she calculated, he was anxious to distance himself from any of what had transpired with his mate. She tried another tack.

"Keith, I'd like to get your fingerprints and a DNA swab if that's OK. We just need it for the purposes of elimination. You've nothing to worry about, and it's voluntary. What do you say?"

Gillespie thought for a moment.

"If it will help me to get clear of all this crap, I'll agree. But don't you dare try and use it against me," he said defiantly.

"Of course not. Despite what you might think, Keith, we don't fit people up with crimes here in Galway. We much prefer to arrest the actual perpetrators!"

"Whatever," Gillespie said, clearly unconvinced.

Lyons took out the swab kit that she carried in her inside jacket pocket and asked Gillespie to open his mouth wide. She ran the long white stick around the inside of his cheek and withdrew it, placing it into the plastic tube and sealing it. It wasn't technically correct to do this out in the wilderness with no witnesses, but it was the best she could achieve, and it was more for show than anything else. As she was doing it, she imagined what a good defence lawyer would have to say about her methods if it ever came to court.

In another jacket pocket she had the Digi-check mobile fingerprint machine, which was no bigger than a rather thick mobile phone. She got Keith to roll his four fingers and thumb along the glass screen on the front of the device, recording his prints. Later, she would transmit the recording using Wi-Fi into the Garda PULSE system where Keith Gillespie's fingerprints would be stored for all time.

"You're still using Terry's phone, Keith," Lyons said as she was putting the paraphernalia away, "how do you come to have it?"

"He left it in the gaff, didn't he?"

"When was this?"

"About ten days ago – the last time I seen him. He said he was going out for a while. I was well hungover, so I didn't pay any attention. But I think he might have had another phone. I seen him with one, I think. Not this one."

"I'd like to borrow that phone, Keith. Just for a day or two till we can download the call records and check them out," Lyons said.

"Not bleeding likely! What am I supposed to do? I need it for when McGuire has some more work for us."

Lyons didn't want to push the man too far. They could get the call records for Terry's phone from the airtime provider in any case, but there could be text messages or photographs on it that would give some clue to Halpin's demise, and she needed to examine its contents.

"Tell you what. Why don't I give you a different phone. We can swap the SIM cards over, so you get to keep the number and all the contacts, and I'll just take Terry's one. The one I have is better than this one anyway. What do you say?"

"This better not be a trick," Gillespie said.

Lyons took the spare, second phone that she had with her out of yet another pocket in her jacket. It was a spare that they kept in the office, and as such had no personal data in it at all, and just a couple of numbers for a few of the Garda stations around and about. She showed it to Gillespie.

"Look. You take this one – it's a much better spec than Terry's. You can keep it. It's not locked to any particular airtime provider, so it will work with any of them."

"You can use it to track me, I suppose."

"We can do that anyway, Keith, no matter what phone you are using. This one has nothing special about it. It's just a spare we carry in case we lose our own phone, or someone takes it off us."

Lyons could see that Keith was attracted to the new device. It was a much better item than the one Terry had been using.

"OK, then. And then I'm off."

"Yes, and thanks for your co-operation."

They fiddled with the mobile phones till Keith was equipped with the new one, loaded with the SIM card from Terry Halpin's phone, and Lyons took the instrument and dropped it into a small plastic evidence bag.

"You stay here for ten minutes now while I get clear. No messing. OK?"

"Yes, OK, Keith."

When Gillespie had left, Lyons called Pascal Brosnan and told him what was happening.

"Don't try to follow him, Pascal, we can keep an eye on him through the phone. Let him think he's got clean away. I'll come up to you in a few minutes."

"OK, Inspector, we'll wait here."

When Lyons had waited a few minutes, she got up and left the old ruin, casting a wistful glance back at the place as she walked briskly up the road.

"That place has seen some drama," she said to herself, remembering the man who lived there with his wife just a few years back, before he had become besotted by a Polish escort girl.

Chapter Twenty-two

"Are you going back to Galway, Inspector?" Pascal Brosnan asked when the four of them were together up beside Mary Fallon's car at the bridge in Ballyconneely.

"No, Pascal, I want to go into Clifden and pay a quick call on Sergeant Mulholland. I don't like working his patch without dropping in to see him."

"Could you give me a lift in then?" Brosnan said. "I have something I need to tell him too."

* * *

"Ah, hello, Maureen," Séan Mulholland greeted Lyons as she came into the station with Brosnan in tow. "I heard you were out this way. Can I get you a cuppa?"

"No thanks, Séan, I just wanted to drop in and say hello. I brought Pascal with me – he has something he wants to talk to you about."

"Oh, fair enough. What's on your mind, Pascal?" Mulholland said.

Brosnan looked nervously at Lyons and back to Mulholland and seemed reluctant to speak.

"Ah, go on with ye. You can say anything that has to be said in front of the inspector. She's one of us," Mulholland said, sensing the young Garda's hesitancy.

"Right you are. Well, you see, Mary and I were out at Kilnatrá yesterday." He went on to recite the situation they had observed with the van unloading what looked like smuggled drink into the back of the pub.

"I thought you might like to have a word with the owner of the place yourself, Sergeant. What do you think?"

"Aye, it might be best. Did you get the number of the van?"

"I did of course. And I managed to get a photograph of the driver too. I was a bit away, but I reckon it could be enhanced."

"Good man, Pascal. Send it on to Inspector Lyons here and she'll take it back to Galway and get it processed."

Lyons, who had remained silent whilst Pascal Brosnan was telling the tale to his sergeant, intervened.

"Pascal, do you think this could have anything to do with Halpin's death?"

"God, I don't know. Maybe. Possibly he knew what was going on, and tried to muscle in on it – get a cut of the proceeds or something. But it seems a bit unlikely. Wasn't he getting a good amount from whatever he was up to with McGuire?"

"Yes, but if, as you say, he was trying to scam the scammers, they could have got spooked and seen him off. Those northern thugs don't think twice about doing serious damage to someone," Mulholland said. "Why don't you let me have a word with Cathal McDermott? I can put the wind up him. I have a few other bits and pieces I can throw at him to loosen his tongue."

Lyons looked at Mulholland and raised her left eyebrow.

"Ah, 'twas something and nothing. He was using a car for a few months last year. Turns out it was down from the North. No VRT paid on it or anything, and then we learnt it had a slightly chequered history. I had a word and he gave it to Deasy to break the next day. So he owes me, if you see what I mean," Mulholland said with not a hint of irony.

"Right, Séan. You do that, and let me know what he says. I'm sure he knows more than he's told us so far in any case. Are you done here, Pascal? Do you want a lift back to Roundstone?"

"Thanks, Inspector, but is that not taking you out of your way?"

"No, not at all. I enjoy the road around by the coast. Shall we?"

* * *

"Have you known the sergeant long, Inspector?" Brosnan asked as they drove out along the old bog road towards Roundstone.

"I sure have. Seems like a lifetime. We were both sergeants together at one time, and we worked a good few tricky cases. He has a great nose for a policeman. That's more valuable than any amount of procedure and book learning in this business."

"I'm beginning to see what you mean. But do his unconventional ways not bother you sometimes?"

"No, they don't, Pascal. We have to remember that we are here to serve the population, not terrorize them. Did you know that Clifden has the lowest crime rate in the whole Western Region? I'm not saying that's all down to Séan Mulholland, but I'll wager he and his unconventional ways have something to do with it."

"But take that business with McDermott and the Northern Ireland car. Would it not have been right to prosecute him?"

"Maybe. But some fast talking solicitor could have convinced the judge that it was his brother's car, and that it was just being used for tourism in the south, or at worst, McDermott would have got a fine and the car taken off him. Then you have an enemy with a grudge working against you. He lost the car anyway – Séan saw to that – and now he can use the episode as leverage to uncover something much more sinister. See what I mean?"

"Hmm, I suppose so. I guess I still have a bit to learn, Inspector, about policing in the wild west."

"Don't ever stop learning, Pascal. Every day brings something new. I could have lifted yer man Gillespie today – I would have been quite within my rights to arrest him as a person of interest. But I'd prefer to have him out and about mixing with whatever low life he's involved with. We'll learn more from that than we would having him banged up in a cell saying 'no comment' in response to every question we asked him. Right now he thinks I'm some kind of a pushover – an easy mark. That's a good place to have him coming from."

"I think Gillespie might be making a mistake there, Inspector."

"Let's hope so, Pascal, let's hope so."

* * *

Lyons dropped Brosnan off at the Garda station in Roundstone and set off back to Galway. It was mid-afternoon by the time she got to Mill Street, parked her car and went into her office. The sky had clouded over, and judging by the moist breeze whistling down the street, there would be rain later. But Lyons had more important things on her mind.

As soon as she got inside, she detected a buzz in the air, and everyone seemed to be at full stretch. She stopped by Eamon Flynn's desk, and invited him into her office.

"Well, Eamon, what's been going on?"

Chapter Twenty-three

"Hi, boss. Dr Dodd wants you to call him. He seems to have some information that he's only willing to divulge to the SIO," Flynn said, barely managing to keep the indignation out of his voice.

"I'll give him a call in a minute. Anything else?"

"Yes, there is. Pascal Brosnan put the number of a van he spotted out at Kilnatrá into the system earlier, and guess what?" Flynn said.

"What?"

"It's very similar to the registration that once belonged to the burnt-out van that was found at Lough Bollard. And what's more, they are both fake. They belong to old bangers that were scrapped in the mid-nineties. What do you make of that?"

"I'm not sure. Does that mean that we have established a connection between the Halpin killing and the body in the van?" Lyons said.

"Not necessarily. But there's something going on that involves that pub, the two deaths and for my money McGuire as well," Flynn said.

"Sounds like it OK, but what?"

Flynn offered no opinion.

"I'd better give the good doctor a call. Let's hope he's in better humour than the last time I spoke to him."

Lyons dialled the number for Dr Julian Dodd, who answered promptly.

"Dr Dodd. It's Inspector Lyons. You were looking for me."

"Ah, yes, Inspector. Thanks for calling back. It's about the body that was found out at Lough Bollard. We've been working hard to try and establish the time of death," Dodd said.

"Surely we know that. Wasn't he killed a few days before the old guy found him?"

"That was the conclusion everyone jumped to, but if I had been called out as I should have been to examine the body in situ, we could have come to a different position more quickly."

"How's that, Doctor?" Lyons said.

"Well, he was set alight on the night before he was discovered, that's almost certain. But he had been dead for quite a number of days before that, maybe more than a week, if I'm not very much mistaken."

"I see. How certain are you?"

"I'd stake my reputation on it, Inspector."

"I see. And what about the cause of death, Doctor?"

"His skull had been smashed in. His head is very badly burnt, but the injury is clearly visible. The bone wasn't destroyed by the fire, so the wound is quite obvious to the experienced eye."

"Can you give any idea of the actual date or time of death?"

"It's very difficult in these cases. We're doing some work on the larvae adhering to the small amount of flesh that wasn't burnt on the lower right leg. When Sinéad's finished that, we'll have a better idea. I'll get her to call you."

"Thanks, yes, please do. Bye."

* * *

When Lyons had finished talking to the pathologist, and Eamon Flynn had left her office, she called Hays.

"Hi, Mick. It's me. Listen, you wouldn't by any chance be free to attend another briefing down here in about half an hour, would you?"

"Maybe. What's up?" Hays said.

"This Halpin thing seems to be going round and round in circles. We are all still having trouble getting a grip on it. I'd welcome your experienced view on how to try and crack it."

"OK. But I don't want to undermine your position as SIO. I'll just be my usual cool self, and stand at the back of the room. How's that?"

"Excellent, Superintendent! See you in half an hour."

Lyons then went to find John O'Connor, who told her he'd been able to trace the shoe from the body in the burnt-out van back to the shop in Malta, but that they didn't appear to have a record of who'd bought it. She gave him the phone that Gillespie had reluctantly handed over, and told him to get busy with it.

"You know the drill, John. I want the full monty on this one. Calls, texts, pictures, incoming and outgoing for as far back as you can. And get onto the airtime provider too to flesh it out a bit. And don't let them put you off with any of that data protection nonsense. If they start that, put them onto me."

"OK, boss. I'll get on it straight away."

The next call Lyons made was to Sinéad Loughran at the lab.

"Hi, Sinéad. Listen, I'm having a briefing here in about half an hour. The superintendent is going to attend. We really need to make some progress with these two deaths. Could you come across and bring whatever information you have from your investigation of the bodies with you?"

"Yes, of course. Have you had some kind of a breakthrough, Maureen?"

"No. Quite the opposite. But I'm hoping if we all give it a good rattle, we'll come up with something new. This is doing my head in."

"OK. See you in half an hour then. Cheers."

* * *

Thirty minutes later and they were all assembled in the open plan. Hays had, as he said he would, slipped in at the back of the room and was standing close to the door doing his best to be invisible. Lyons kicked off the meeting by summarizing the state of play.

"As far as jigsaw puzzles go, this is a cracker! Now, has anyone got anything useful to add?" she said when she had brought them up to date.

Sinéad Loughran was the first to speak.

"Inspector, I have done some detailed analysis on the body from the van. I've concentrated on the development of the maggots that were living on the piece of the victim's leg that hadn't been destroyed. It looks as if the guy in the van was actually killed before Terry Halpin, unless I'm very much mistaken."

"Shit! Are you sure, Sinéad, because if that's the case, there's a whole lot more questions that need answering, like where was the body being kept up until the time the van was set alight?"

"It's certainly looking that way, Inspector. I'll confirm it to you once I have finished my analysis."

"I see. Well thanks for that! So, could Halpin have killed the guy in the van, and if so, who transported him to the field up at Lough Bollard and set him alight? And why wait more than a week to do it? Jesus, this gets worse by the minute. Have you anything on Halpin's phone, John?"

"Not yet, I'm afraid. All I've seen so far is a lot of local calls coming and going. Quite a few to McGuire's place, and several to an unregistered burner. Those ones lasted a long time generally – sometimes over half an hour," O'Connor said.

"Have you more to do on it?" Lyons asked.

"Yes. I'm waiting for the records from the phone company, but there's no sign of any long-distance calls to Malta – not that I can see anyway."

"OK, John, thanks. Stay with it till you get the full story. Eamon, have you anything further on McGuire?"

"No, boss. He's dodgy – we know that – but he just seems to be a developer of sorts with a brother that lives in Malta. He visits him two or three times a year. The brother is in import-export, or so McGuire told me."

"That often covers a multitude. I'd love to know what Ardal McGuire's business really entails. Anyone any ideas?"

"I could fly out there for a week or two and have a look around for you, boss," Sally Fahy volunteered, raising a laugh from everyone in the room.

"Thanks, Sally, but I was thinking of something a little less expensive," Lyons said, looking at Hays.

"I might be able to help," Hays said from the back of the room. "I could give the police in Malta a call and ask if they have any information on McGuire's brother – if he's known to them, or whatever. It's a bit of a long shot – but you never know."

"Do you have any contacts out there, sir?" Lyons said.

"Not really. I did meet an inspector from the Maltese police at a Europol conference in Copenhagen a couple of years ago. I think I may have the details somewhere. I could look him up for you."

"Thanks. That would be great. And see if they are missing a twenty-something-year-old male citizen while you're at it. It looks as if the body in the van could have been Maltese. Meanwhile, Eamon, I want you to dig much deeper into the local Mr McGuire. Bank accounts, properties, business deals, newspaper articles, family – other than his brother – everything you can. Get a warrant if you have to. I want him to know we are digging."

"OK, boss. Will you sign that off for us, Superintendent?" Flynn asked, turning to look at the senior officer.

"Yes, of course. I was about to suggest it myself in any case. You know what I always say – follow the money!" Hays said.

"Great, thanks. Now, Sally. I want you to hook up with Pascal Brosnan and look into this business at the pub. There seems to be a connection between the van that Pascal saw delivering bootleg booze to the place, and the van that the body was found in. Talk to Séan Mulholland, but make it clear we need to question the publican to see what he knows. I want the identity of the driver of the delivery van, and a location for him, or at the very least, when his next delivery is taking place. And warn McDermott not to tip him off if he wants to keep his license – OK?" Lyons said.

"Right, boss. I'll give Sergeant Mulholland a call first thing tomorrow – well maybe not too early!" Sally said, raising another titter from the group.

Chapter Twenty-four

When the briefing was over, Mick Hays and Maureen Lyons retired to her office.

"Ok, Mick, now tell me what you really think," Lyons said, sitting down behind her desk.

"I think it would be very easy to get too focused on the Maltese connection, and Mr McGuire and his brother. After all, it's quite far-fetched to think that someone would come all the way over here and get into some kind of a scrap and end up cremated out on the bog. But I know the evidence, such as it is, is pointing that way at the moment. But if I were you, I'd try and broaden it out a bit. The whole scenario as we know it just now is all a bit neat for my liking. To use that horrible expression 'try thinking outside the box'."

"Hmm... I see what you mean about it all being a bit one track, but we have no other connections to anything else at the moment."

"No, I know that. But have you checked to see if Terry Halpin ever visited Malta, say, in the last twelve months?"

"No, I hadn't thought of that," Lyons said.

"Well there's only Air Malta and Ryanair on the route from Dublin, so why not get them to search their records and see if anything pops up. I'll give that guy in Malta a call tomorrow and see if he comes up with anything. Oh, and have you considered that there may be more than one thing going on here?"

"What do you mean?"

"Well there's the smuggled hooch at the bar in Kilnatrá, apart altogether from the two murders. Your team seem to have joined the dots – you know, two plus two equals six, sort of thing. The link is pretty tenuous."

"You mean the vans' registration numbers?"

"Yes, exactly. Who do we know that could fix up a few random sets of plates in these parts if the price was right?" Hays said.

"Deasy! Do you think he could be involved?"

"Possibly. I doubt if he's mixed up with the killings, but it would be worth paying a social call on him over the vans. I'd probably be able to come out with you tomorrow if you needed someone heavy to lean on him a bit."

"Ah, you're grand, Mick. Anyway, you're not that much overweight!" Lyons said smiling.

"Feck off, Inspector. Remember you are speaking to a senior officer," Hays said.

Lyons got up from her seat and came round to where Hays was sitting. She leaned in and planted a long soft kiss on his willing lips.

"I love it when you're all masterful, sir!" she said when they had disengaged.

"OK. Let's get out of here. What do you fancy to eat?" Hays said.

"I'll rustle up something at home. I'm too buggered to go out anywhere, anyway there's good telly tonight."

"Right. Get your jacket and let's go."

* * *

On the way out to Salthill in Hays' car – Lyons had decided to leave hers in the station car park overnight –

Hays asked her about the little house in the city that she was thinking of buying.

"Any news on your property dealings?" he said.

"Oh, yes, I forgot to tell you in all the madness. I had a call from Sheila. She's spoken to Séamus, and she says they can let me have thirty grand out of the farm. I think it's too much, but she's insistent. She says they'll still have good reserves, and if they fall on hard times, they can ask me for help," Lyons said.

"Nice one. Is she still insisting it's not a loan?"

"Yes. It's to do with my shareholding in the place. Séamus says he can get his accountant to work out the details so there shouldn't be much tax, if any, to pay on it. Apparently, if it's re-invested straight away, then the tax is deferred till the final transaction happens – whatever that is."

"Sounds good. Have you got the other thirty?"

"Not all of it. But I'll get a small loan from the Credit Union to make it up and then we should be good to go. What about your half? Have you got it in readies, or will you have to sell something?"

"No. I have it in a savings account with instant access, so I can get at it quickly. What's the next step?" Hays said.

"I'll get onto the owner and tell him we have a deal, and then we'll need a solicitor to start the conveyance. I'll get the place surveyed as well, just in case. I don't suppose you know anyone in that line?" Lyons said.

"I don't, but I know a man that does. I could give James McMahon a call. I'm sure he'd know of a decent surveyor."

"That would be great. Thanks. I'll tell the owner of the place that we're moving on it and to expect to hear from a surveyor shortly, and I'll ask him who his solicitor is. How's that?"

"Sounds good. What's his name anyway?"

"Staunton. Gerry Staunton – retired civil servant. He's really nice."

* * *

The following morning when all the detectives had gone about their busy day, Hays found himself with a few minutes to spare, so he called Jim McMahon, the architect that they had both met during the investigation of a murder out on the old bog road near Ballyconneely a few years ago.

Hays had stayed in touch with McMahon, who wasn't involved in the case, or at least only in a very peripheral sense, and they met up ever so often for a chat or a spot of lunch. McMahon was very well connected in Galway, and Hays had found him to be useful with information from time to time.

"Oh, hello Mick. I haven't heard from you for a while. Everything OK with you?" McMahon said when Hays got through to him.

"Yes, thanks, James. Sorry to disturb you, but Maureen and I are contemplating buying a property here in the city, and we need a good surveyor to give the place a thorough once over. It looks to be in good shape, but you never know what's lurking in the rafters. It's pretty old."

"That's no problem. We have an eager young guy working for us here as it happens. He's very sound. If there's a woodworm hiding anywhere in the place – he'll find it! His name is Robert Neary – shall I get him to give you a call?"

"Yes, thanks, James. That would be smashing, and you can send the fee note directly to me. I gather you're keeping busy then?" Hays said.

"Run off our feet to be honest, Mick. There's an awful lot of new money pouring into Galway these days, and an awful lot of run-down property that needs refurbishing, thank heavens."

"Hmm... interesting. Have you ever come across a guy by the name of Senan McGuire?"

"Bloody hell, I sure have! Enough to stay well away from him in any case. He's trouble that one."

"Oh. How come?"

"Word has it that he's mixed up with some iffy foreigners who seem to have more money than sense. I heard that he'd let out that old broken down place on Market Street for an outrageous rent – something like ten thousand a month – but that could be exaggerated. And he's buying fixer-uppers for stupid money, too. Sending all the local guys into orbit."

"Wow. So, you haven't had any dealings with him yourselves then?" Hays said.

"Not likely. We can afford to be quite choosy these days about who we do business with."

"Well, look that's great, James. Many thanks. I'll expect a call from Robert then, and we must have a drink or lunch someday soon – do a real catch up."

"Sounds good, Mick. Give me a call when you have a free slot. Cheers."

Hays parked the information he had found out about Senan McGuire. It would be interesting to see if Eamon Flynn got the same story from McGuire's accounts and bank transactions.

Hays then took out a box of filing containing papers that went back a couple of years. He found what he needed two-thirds of the way down through the pile.

"Ah, here we are. Let's see now – who was there from Malta?" He thumbed his way through the plastic folder relating to the conference he had attended in Copenhagen. He soon found the delegate list.

"Inspector Kristoff Poulis – there you go. I knew I had it somewhere," he said out loud to no one in particular.

Helpfully, Inspector Poulis' phone number was listed on the registration sheet for the conference, so Hays sat down and dialled.

Chapter Twenty-five

"Good morning, Sergeant Mulholland. It's Detective Sally Fahy here from Galway. Inspector Lyons asked me to give you a call. I'm planning on driving out to Kilnatrá this morning and meeting up with Pascal Brosnan to talk to Cathal McDermott at the pub. I was wondering if you'd like to come too?"

"Eh... wait just a minute now, Sally. Has something else happened?" Mulholland said.

"No, but we think there may be a connection between the van that delivers smuggled drink to the pub, and the van that was found burnt out at Lough Bollard with the dead body inside. We need to identify the driver of the booze van and question him."

"I see. Well I think between yourself and Pascal you'll be able to manage without my input. And I can always stay out of it for now and clear up the mess later, if you see what I mean," the wily old sergeant said chuckling to himself. "In any case, I can't really leave the station here unattended during the day."

"OK, but I need to know that you're happy with the plan, Sergeant," Fahy said.

"Ah, you're grand. Do you want me to give Pascal a call and tell him you'll be out to him?"

"Yes, please. It would sound better coming from you, if you don't mind."

"Give me a few minutes then, and I'll ring him. I'm just finishing off a cup of tea," Mulholland said.

"Thanks, Sergeant Mulholland. I'll be out for Pascal in about forty-five minutes."

* * *

Sally Fahy signed out one of the marked Garda cars from the pool and located the white Hyundai estate in the car park to the rear of Mill Street station. She normally took her own car on these missions, but today, she wanted things to look as formal as possible to see if they could put a bit of pressure on Cathal McDermott.

It was a day of mixed blessings as far as the weather, and the traffic was concerned. From time to time heavy showers produced large sheets of rain falling vertically from the heavens and creating pools at the sides of the road where the drains were temporarily overpowered by the volume of water. But in between the showers, the sun shone brightly overhead, and then the road steamed dry in a few minutes, and it got very warm.

The traffic was another matter. The N59 out through Moycullen was busy – busier than Fahy had expected for a mid-week morning. There was construction taking place at Rosscahill – halfway between Moycullen and Oughterard – and muddy sand lorries, JCBs and even a large yellow dumper were all lumbering along the narrow road, bouncing wildly at times on the uneven surface. Fahy had to stay tucked in behind the convoy or risk overtaking in a dangerous manner, which she didn't want to do. She wondered as she sat there, her pristine white car getting splattered with mud thrown up from the enormous wheels of the construction vehicles, if all of the plant was road legal and had tax and insurance in place – but that was a matter for the uniformed folks, so she quickly banished the thought from her mind.

It was almost half past eleven when she pulled her car into the car park of the small Garda station at Roundstone to see Pascal Brosnan and Mary Fallon sitting outside in the sunshine nursing mugs of tea.

"God, it's well for some," Fahy said getting out of the car.

"There ye are, Sergeant. It looks like you've driven across the fields to get here. Would you like a cuppa?" Brosnan said standing up.

"No thanks. We'd best get on. We'll leave Mary in charge here, and you come with me to Kilnatrá, Pascal. Did Sergeant Mulholland call you?"

"He did to be sure. Apparently, I have to put on my most severe official face for this one!"

"Right. Let's go!"

* * *

Fahy decided to take the road around by Carna to get to the pub, rather than going via Cool Lodge and Lightford. There wasn't a lot in it in terms of time, but Fahy preferred the scenery on the coastal route.

The car park at Tigh Oisrí was sparsely populated with just a handful of cars and a single camper van. The publican allowed one or two of these to park there overnight, and provided an outside tap for fresh water to facilitate the tourists. They invariably had at least one meal in the pub during their stay, and sometimes more, so it was a good deal as far as the pub was concerned.

Fahy pulled the squad car up in front of the door, and both she and Brosnan got out and went inside.

Cathal McDermott was behind the bar, dusting the bottles that were suspended in the optics, and arranging the various implements that were used to prepare lemons and other additions used for the more exotic libations.

"Mr McDermott, we'd like to talk to you for a few minutes, in private please," Fahy said with as much authority as she could summon.

"It's not a very good time. We're just coming up to lunchtime. Would you like to have something and I could talk to you after?"

"I'm sorry, sir, but we're very busy today and we need to get on. Where can we talk privately?" Fahy said.

McDermott sighed, throwing down his duster petulantly, and leading the two officers into the back of the premises where there was an office of sorts.

"Right," McDermott said, folding his arms and lounging back against the bookcase that lined one wall of the small room. "What do you want?"

"It has been observed that you are taking deliveries of stock from a van that is registered in Northern Ireland. Would you like to tell us about that, Mr McDermott?" Fahy said.

"So what?"

"What, Mr McDermott, is that the van that brings this stock to your premises is driving on false plates. The registration belongs to a vehicle that was written off during the 1990s."

"That's nothing to do with me. It's not my van."

"We're not suggesting that it is, but we need to know the names of the firms that are supplying all your drink here, and we also need the name of the man that delivers in the blue Northern Ireland registered van," Brosnan said.

"You can look at my books. You'll see it's all in order," McDermott said sourly.

"It's not your books that interest us. It's what's being done off the books we want to know about. Now, who is the delivery man?"

McDermott said nothing, looking down at the floor.

"Very well. I'm afraid we're going to have to arrest you and bring you in to Roundstone Garda station," Fahy said.

"You can't do that. I have to serve at the bar. Herself can't manage on her own."

"Well then, you'd better start talking, Mr McDermott. And as I said we are very busy, so don't keep me waiting!" Fahy said, a little surprised at the officiousness of her demands.

"OK, OK. The man you want is Cónan O'Neill. I have a mobile number for him I can give you."

"Where does he live?" Brosnan asked.

"I've no idea. He just comes and delivers the stuff and I pay him in cash – that's it."

"Where does he get the drink?" Fahy said.

"Search me. With that kind of transaction, you don't ask too many questions. But I can tell you that some of the spirits are from the UK. It says it on the labels. I decant those into Irish bottles so as not to raise eyebrows," McDermott said.

"How long has this being going on?" Brosnan said.

"A while now." When neither of the Gardaí said anything, McDermott went on, "maybe two years or so."

"Right. Pascal, will you go with Mr McDermott here and collect a few bottles of the bootleg spirits. Give him a receipt, and bag them up as evidence."

McDermott led the way out of the office and Brosnan followed, leaving Fahy behind to have a root around amongst the paperwork that was strewn about on the desk. After a few minutes, having found nothing particularly interesting, she followed the other two out into the bar.

"One more thing, Mr McDermott. If you make any attempt to contact Cónan O'Neill before we have spoken to him – any attempt at all by phone, text, or email, I will close this place down in a heartbeat and arrest you for perverting the course of justice. Is that clear?"

McDermott grunted, but said nothing.

"Have you got the samples and O'Neill's number, Pascal?"

"Yes, Sarge, all bagged up and recorded."

"Right, let's get out of here."

Chapter Twenty-six

"Hello, Kristoff. It's Mick Hays from Ireland here. Remember? We met at that conference in Copenhagen?"

"Ah, Mick, yes of course. How could I forget. You taught me how to drink whiskey – too much whiskey. It must be two years at least. What have you been up to?"

"Just all the usual nonsense, Kristoff, and you?"

"Same here. It's getting much harder to be a policeman in Malta though. There are a lot of difficult things going on. Anyway, what can I do for you?" Poulis said.

"We're in the middle of an investigation here involving a Senan McGuire. He has a brother, Ardal, who lives on Malta. Runs some sort of import-export company. I don't suppose you know anything about him?" Hays said.

"McGuire – yes, I do indeed. We have been keeping a close eye on him for some time, but he's slippery – very slippery. He mixes in the wrong kind of circles, if you know what I mean. Friends in low places – all very wealthy, of course. And he is supposed to be in import-export, but he doesn't seem to import or export anything. Every time we seem to be getting close to him, we get warned off – told to leave it. Why, what do you know?"

Hays went on to tell the Maltese inspector about the discovery of the dead man in the van out at Lough Bollard, and the Maltese euros that they found in the bedsit belonging to the other victim.

"That doesn't really surprise me. We have an awful lot of hot money flowing through Malta at the moment. It's coming from all over, and it's very hard to stop it. And, I don't wish to be disrespectful, but the Irish banks have a reputation for light-touch regulation, so it wouldn't surprise me if your banking system was being used to wash some of it clean."

Hays was a bit uncomfortable with what Poulis had said.

"Have you any evidence for any of this, Kristoff?"

"No, I'm afraid not. But it does sort of make sense. But you say that the lad in the van was Maltese. Any identification?"

"No, none, I'm afraid. Just a shoe that we traced back to a shop in Valletta."

"Could you send me over all the details of the body that you found, especially the shoe and the money too? I might be able to find out something from this end. I'll have a look to see if we are missing one of our citizens as well – although, to be honest, that's not terribly unusual these days. Quite a few disappear – especially if they fall foul of the organised criminals."

"Sounds like you have your hands full, Kristoff."

"I try and stay out of it. They have recently formed a special squad to try and get to grips with organised crime on the island, but I'm not very hopeful."

"Hmm... OK. Well, I'll gladly send over whatever we have, and if you could get back to me if you find anything out."

The men exchanged mobile phone numbers and email addresses.

"Thanks very much, Kristoff. I look forward to hearing from you."

"Yes, yes of course, and if you get a chance to come across to Malta at any stage, I'd be happy to show you around."

"Thanks, Kristoff. Talk soon."

When Hays had finished the call, he went in search of Eamon Flynn whom he found pouring over a hot PC with several official-looking screens open.

"Eamon! Just the man I was looking for."

Hays relayed the conversation he had had with Poulis in Malta and asked if Flynn had discovered anything sinister in McGuire's records.

"Yes, sir, I have. His accounts are fascinating. You know that old, closed-up shop on Market Street? Well, according to the records, it's let, and bringing in over €4,000 a month in rent. And that's not all. Several of his other fixer-uppers are allegedly rented out too, and he has a rent roll of almost fifty grand a month coming in."

"Inter-es-ting. Any idea where all the money is going?" Hays said.

"It goes back out. He's paying out serious money to sub-contractors. I've just started investigating one or two, and it looks like they are bogus."

"Who are the tenants?"

"That's the odd thing. They're all foreign companies. They're from all over – Spain, Italy and so on," Flynn said.

"Any of them from Malta?"

"No. not yet anyway. Look, do you think I could get a bit of a hand with this, sir? Maybe someone from the forensic accountancy lot."

"Stay at it for now, Eamon. We need to keep this tight till we find out what's going on. See if you can build a path of where the money is coming from and going to, and of course how much is involved, and how often. Did Maureen get anything from the airlines about Gillespie?"

"I'm not sure, sir. I'll check with her when she gets back," Flynn said.

"Where is she anyway?" Hays said.

"I think herself and Mary Fallon are calling on Tadgh Deasy, sir."

"Oh, right. Well, if you see her, ask her to give me a call. I have to go to a meeting now. Can you send this stuff across to an Inspector Poulis in Malta for me. Here's the details of what he wants, and his email address."

"Yes, sure, no problem."

* * *

As Fahy drove back from Kilnatrá towards Roundstone with Pascal Brosnan, the signal on her mobile phone was fading in and out.

"Damn this thing!" she exclaimed. "Why can't they give us decent equipment – this is hopeless."

"It's always the same out here. Even in Roundstone it can be patchy enough. It's quite a risk to us when we are on a tricky operation. Maybe we should ask them to give us all satellite phones like the coastguard have," Brosnan said.

"I can just see Superintendent Hays' face when that request goes in, he'd have a bloody conniption. Why don't you raise it with him?"

"Ha ha, very funny. No, I think I'll leave that to Inspector Lyons!"

By the time they got to the Garda station in Roundstone, Sally Fahy had had second thoughts about trying to call Cónan O'Neill in any case. She felt it might be better to bring the information back to Galway with her and seek advice from Lyons as to how best to play it.

She said goodbye to Pascal Brosnan and headed back to town.

Chapter Twenty-seven

"I hear you're getting on very well with Pascal," Lyons said to Mary Fallon as they drove out from Roundstone towards Tadgh Deasy's garage.

Mary didn't quite know how to respond to that, so she said nothing.

"He's a really nice guy. I don't blame you. But, Mary, you need to be really careful."

"Nothing has happened," Fallon said defensively.

"OK, I hear you, but if it were to take off, it could easily ruin both your careers. These things rarely end well – trust me, I've seen it many times."

"Do you mind if I say something, boss?"

"Sure."

"You and the superintendent seem to have made it work."

"Yes, I know, and to be brutally honest, I'm more surprised than anyone else about that. It should be a train wreck, but it just works. We've talked about it a lot, and neither of us can figure it out. But I promise you, it's very much the exception."

"Who told you and what did they say? We haven't even kissed for heaven's sake."

"You were spotted holding hands, that's all."

"Shit! That was part of an undercover thing. But I think we both enjoyed being close all the same. He really is a good bloke," Fallon said.

"Well, we've had 'the talk', so it's up to you how you handle it. You're a good-looking girl, Mary. You could have your pick. Just don't risk your career. We need good cops like yourself and Pascal in the force."

"Maybe I'll just set my cap at Séan Mulholland then!" she said and the two of them laughed out loud.

* * *

Lyons pulled her car into Deasy's yard and brought it to a halt. Deasy, as usual, had his head stuck under the bonnet of some hopeless jalopy, trying to breathe life into it. When he saw Lyons arrive, he stood back from the car he was working on. He was dressed in filthy overalls, and had oily black hands where he was working without vinyl gloves on the vehicle.

"Good morning, ladies," he said trying to be cheerful, though he was less than pleased to see the two of them, "what can I do for you today?"

"Hello, Tadgh. We just need a word."

As Lyons engaged the man in conversation about the two vans in which the Gardaí had an interest, Mary Fallon went walkabout to see what she could observe.

Lyons started her questions with the blue van that was delivering to the pub out at Kilnatrá.

"What do you know of a Northern-registered blue Transit that delivers drink around these parts?"

"I don't know nothing. I haven't sold a Transit for at least two years. Good ones are hard to come by," Deasy said.

"Maybe the guy just wanted a set of plates. Would you know anything about that at all?"

"Definitely not. Where would I get those?"

"Tadgh, when we get to talk to the driver of the blue van – and we will – I hope for your sake he backs up your story. This is serious. Two people have died, and we can't just brush this one under the carpet, so if you know anything about any of this, it would be better if you told us now."

Deasy looked down at his boots, and said nothing.

"Boss. Over here," Mary Fallon called from the door of a smaller shed at the side of the main workshop. She had initially thought that it was a toilet, but as she pushed the door open cautiously, she could see that she was mistaken.

Lyons walked over to where Mary Fallon was holding some plastic film in her hand. Inside the shed, there was a number plate making machine. A stack of white and yellow plates were stored beneath the rough wooden bench.

Lyons held up the waste that Fallon had found and saw that it was a sort of stencil where numbers had been stamped out, and she recognised the numbers that had been formed as those belonging to the blue van seen at Tigh Oisrí.

Lyons instructed Fallon to bag the evidence and she went back to where Deasy was standing looking dejected.

"Right, Tadgh. Start talking, or I'll have to take you in."

"Ah, it's nothing. A fella came in with the van and said he had a lot of parking tickets and speeding fines on its registration, and asked me if I could sort him out. That's all."

"So, you just thought you'd stamp out some random NI number and fit them to his van, is that it?"

"He gave me the number. I don't know nothing about these things."

"Yeah, right. Did this guy have a name?" Lyons asked.

"He never said."

"And how much did he pay you to break the law, Tadgh?"

"He didn't. He gave me three bottles of whiskey from the back of the van. They'd be worth fifty quid or more, so I wasn't unhappy."

"We'll have to take those I'm afraid. They are evidence, and besides the duty hasn't been paid on them, so it's best if we relieve you of them. Is that the extent of your involvement, Tadgh? Truth now."

"Yes, of course."

"You didn't supply the van?"

"No. Of course not."

"Hmm... I hope you're telling the truth. It will go very badly for you if I find out you've been lying. Oh, and we're taking all your number plate blanks away – they are evidence."

"Ah, God, don't do that, Inspector. I need them for me business."

"Don't push it, Tadgh. I'll give you a receipt!"

The two Gardaí walked around the dirty old yard while Deasy went and got the whiskey. One of the bottles was already half empty, but the other two had not been opened. It really was a bit of a dump. Old, crashed cars lay rusting here and there with their major parts removed. Over at one side of the yard, a tired-looking beige Toyota Corolla sat with a 'For Sale' sign in the window, offering the vehicle for the princely sum of €999 'Or Near Offer'. Lyons was thinking €9.99 would be nearer the mark.

After a few minutes, finding nothing to pique their curiosity further, Fallon put the bag of plastic plates and the three whiskey bottles in the boot of her own car and departed.

* * *

On the way back to Roundstone, Mary Fallon asked Lyons, "Do you think he was telling the truth, boss?"

"Not sure. He's a dodgy enough character, and we've caught him out a few times in the past, but he can be useful to us as well, so I don't want to piss him off completely. But I'm not putting up with too much crap from him either. When we get back, will you bring Séan up to speed on what has taken place, and ask him to keep an eye on Deasy's yard for the next few days."

"Yes, sure. It must be hard to make a judgement call in these cases, boss. How do you get it right?"

"I don't always, but when I do, it's down to experience mostly. And instinct. Don't ever go against your gut, Mary. It's the best asset you'll ever have in detecting crime – believe me."

"I'll remember that. God, I have a lot to learn."

"We all have. It never stops."

When they arrived at the Garda station in Roundstone it was still locked up with the usual notice on the door instructing anyone who needed assistance to call Clifden. Mary Fallon opened up, and asked Lyons if she would like a cuppa before setting off back into Galway.

"Yes, thanks. That would be great."

Mary went about boiling the kettle and dishing up two mugs of tea, and she managed to find a few biscuits to accompany the refreshments.

As they sat down, Fallon said, "Thanks for your advice, boss. I appreciate it."

"Ah, don't mind me. I'm not perfect by any means, Mary. But I've seen a lot in my years in the force, and if I can pass some of it on it might be some help. But remember – follow your instinct."

Chapter Twenty-eight

Lyons got back into the city in good time to hold the afternoon briefing. The drive back had been pleasant enough, the plague of slow-moving rental cars that thronged the roads out west not having got properly underway as yet. On the journey, Lyons reflected on the chat she had had with Mary Fallon. It got her to thinking about her own relationship with Mick Hays.

It had started several years back when they were sent to Poland to investigate a murder that had taken place in Ballyconneely. Lyons had been very apprehensive about things going anywhere. Even then, she had seen how affairs in the force could wreck careers, not to mention cause serious disruption to the teams that the participants were working with. But Lyons and her new boyfriend had taken it relatively slowly. And Hays, who was at that time just an inspector, had the good sense to inform his boss quite early on. The man had been horrified initially, but as time went on, and the union of two of his best officers seemed to bring even better results for the team than ever, he softened his approach.

When Lyons had been threatened by a particularly nasty villain who said he knew where she lived, and he was coming for her, she had moved in temporarily with Hays for safety reasons, and they had got on even better as a result. So, as time progressed, and their feelings for each other grew, they decided to make it a permanent arrangement. Lyons still had misgivings, but it had worked really well ever since. They both had their own interests. Lyons was keen on photography, and learning European languages, while Hays had his beloved sailing boat that filled a lot of his meagre leisure time. Lyons had wondered if they would marry, but she wasn't hung up on the idea, and it never seemed to occur to Hays, so she let well alone. They had never discussed the issue of children either, and both of them seemed content to leave it that way. "So far, so good," she said to herself as she swung the Volvo into the yard at Mill Street station.

* * *

The briefing took its usual form with each of the team reporting back on their respective endeavours for the day. Sinéad Loughran had come across to join them too, and Lyons invited her to speak first.

"Firstly," Sinéad said, "I finished the analysis of the bugs we found on Malta Man's lower leg. I ran the results past Dr Dodd as well just to be sure I'm not mistaken, but he confirmed my findings. We are now pretty certain that Malta Man died before Terry Halpin. Also, I had some time on my hands, so I did a fair bit of work on Halpin's clothes. There were some odd stains on his jeans and socks, so I took samples and had them analysed. It turns out that some of it was marine diesel fuel, and the other stuff was traces of marine gearbox oil."

"Could he have picked that kind of thing up when he was in the water?" Lyons said.

"No. The patterns don't suggest that at all. The substances were very local to particular areas on his clothing. If he had just floated through some of that stuff, it would have been all over, and much less concentrated.

No, I'd say your friend was on a boat shortly before he died and got the stains from that. And not a very well-maintained vessel either," Loughran said.

"It's amazing what forensics can tell us these days. Thanks, Sinéad. Anything else?" Lyons said.

"That's it for now."

"OK. Who's next?" Lyons said.

Sally Fahy recounted the visit with Pascal Brosnan to the pub out at Kilnatrá and the conversation that had taken place with Cathal McDermott.

"I hope you didn't call him, Sally?" Lyons said.

"No, boss, of course not. Why? What have you in mind?" Fahy said.

"I'll tell you after. Anything else?"

"No, that's it," Fahy said.

"Right. What about you, Eamon?" Lyons said.

"Well, a few things. I put an enquiry in to the airlines as you suggested, boss. It turns out Terry Halpin did visit Malta – twice as it happens. He went out in September last year, and then again as soon as the flights started again this summer. He stayed a week the first time, and four days the second."

"Interesting. Did he book any accommodation with the flights?" Lyons said.

"No – not on the airline websites in any case. He may have been previously, too, but the airline records don't go back any further, at least not without a warrant and a lot of fuss."

"OK. Good work, Eamon. Anything else?" Lyons said.

"Yes. I've been digging into Senan McGuire's businesses. It's all mad. Looks like the sub-contractors he's allegedly been paying to do up the properties that haven't actually been done up at all are bogus. There's hundreds of thousands washing through his bank accounts, but very little – nothing really – to show for it. I'm getting someone from forensic accounting to help me try and figure it all out, but it's definitely irregular."

"Hmm... do you think we should bring him in for a wee chat?" Lyons said.

"That's up to you, boss. Maybe we should leave it till I have some more information. I'll be in a better position to interrogate him in a day or two," Flynn said.

"OK. But get back onto the two airlines. Ask them to keep a look out for McGuire booking a flight to Malta, and let us know immediately. It wouldn't surprise me if he made a run for it."

"Good idea. What about you, boss? Have you anything for us?"

Lyons went on to describe the visit to Tadgh Deasy, and what herself and Mary Fallon had discovered.

"Do you not think it's time we closed that bugger down, boss?" Flynn said.

"Let's hold on to see what this O'Neill character has to say for himself. And that's interesting information about Terry Halpin's clothes. I want to take that further myself. Eamon, when we're done here, can you step into my office for a minute. Oh, and, everyone, don't breathe a word about this O'Neill fella to anyone – no one at all."

* * *

"Right, Eamon. Let's see if we can plan a little surprise for Mr O'Neill." Lyons went on to outline her plan as they sat in her office out of earshot of the rest of the team.

When she had finished, Flynn went off to set things up, and Lyons went looking for Mick Hays. She found him in his office pouring over a report, and not looking too happy.

"Hi! What's up, Mick? You look as if you've eaten a wasp."

"Ah, ye know. These bloody reports. I don't actually think anyone reads the damn things – but the boss wants them word-perfect before they go off, and of course he wants to be very selective about what they say too. Drives me mad. Anyway, what's happening in your world?"

"I'm working away on this Terry Halpin murder, and the other guy who has become known as Malta Man. Halpin apparently visited Malta a few times in the last year or so. It turns out that he may have been on board a boat recently too. Can you ask around for me and see if any of the boating community know of a connection?"

"Yeah, sure, I'd be glad to. Gives me a break from these awful things anyway. Have you any more information?"

"No. Sinéad found traces of marine diesel and marine lubricants on his clothes and says they couldn't have got there from him just being in the water. I know it's a bit thin, but you never know. We're due a lucky break," Lyons said.

"No problem. I'll make enquiries. I'm sure Peadar will know if there's a seafaring link to the lad. Oh, by the way, that reminds me, I'll be late tonight. I have to go to a presentation for one of the lifeboat guys later on. He's done thirty years with them, and they want to mark the occasion. I won't stay long. Will you be OK on your own this evening?"

"I'll survive – somehow," she said with an impish smile. "If you want collecting because you're too pissed to drive, give me a call."

"No, that won't be necessary. I'll have a designated driver with me as it's an official function. The joys of rank!"

Before Mick Hays left the office, he tried to call Inspector Poulis in Malta, but couldn't get through to him. He didn't leave a message, but he did send an email to the man asking him to see if there was any mention of a Terry Halpin associated with the McGuires.

Lyons didn't feel like going home to an empty house and cooking a meal for one, so she called Sinéad Loughran and asked if she would like to go for a meal after work. Sinéad was delighted. They got on well together. They seemed to share the same rather ironic sense of humour, and although Loughran was a good bit younger than Maureen Lyons, it didn't seem to matter.

Chapter Twenty-nine

Lyons and Loughran went to their favourite bistro just off Shop Street after work. It was called An Béal Bocht, which is Irish for The Poor Mouth. The place was always busy. The bar occupied the front half of the premises, while further back, there were square wooden tables painted in a fashionable grey colour that seated the forty or so covers that the restaurant accommodated. Being well known to the place, they had no trouble getting a table in a relatively quiet spot away from the din at the front. Almost as soon as they had taken their seats, Liam, the head waiter came across with two large laminated menus.

"Good evening, girls," he said as he presented them with the bill of fare, "the specials tonight are pan-fried scallops with a rich cream and fennel sauce, dressed crab and smoked salmon salad or minute steak with a homemade pepper sauce served with peppered potato wedges and creamed spinach."

"Thanks, Liam. Give us a minute, but meantime could we have a bottle of the Louis Jadot Chardonnay and a few olives with some bread to start?"

"Certainly, Sinéad. Coming right up!" He spun away heading back behind the busy bar.

"So, how are things with you, Sinéad?" Lyons said.

"God, it's been mad busy. But hopefully, now that the summer is here, things will quieten down. It's been pretty hectic," Loughran said.

"What's been keeping you going? We haven't brought in many violent death cases for a while."

"Suicides. Did you know, Ireland has the fourth highest suicide rate in Europe for fifteen to twenty-four-year-old males. And Galway seems to get more than its fair share. You probably don't realise it, because they aren't classified as suspicious deaths, so the uniformed cops deal with nearly all of them. But now that the university is going on holidays, it will probably ease back a bit," Loughran said.

"God, I hope so. I didn't know it was that much of a problem. It's very sad. Does it bother you a lot?"

"It's the identification that's the hardest. Usually hard-working parents who haven't really got a clue what's going on in their kids' lives, and of course they are completely destroyed. Apart from that, one dead body is much the same as the next – but they are very sad. Such a waste. And the funny thing is, once they get into their mid-twenties and get a partner, it all seems to go away. I don't know – too much social media if you ask me!"

"On the subject of partners, how's the love life?" Lyons said, smiling.

"Funny you should ask, although, knowing you, you're probably already well aware."

"Aware of what?"

"I had a call from Peadar Tobin – you know that hunky Garda from Clifden – his brother is getting married at the end of next week, and he's only asked me to the wedding as his plus one."

"Cool! Well done you, and no, I wasn't aware. I gave up stalking handsome young Gardaí when I started going with Mick," Lyons said.

"Yeah, right!"

"No, but seriously, Peadar is a real genuine guy. I worked with him during that business at the pony show, and he was very thoughtful and considerate, as well as being more or less drop-dead gorgeous, of course. Should I buy a new hat?" Lyons said.

"Feck off, Maureen. We haven't even been out together yet! Of course, I've nothing to wear, so I suppose it will cost me an absolute fortune. Bang goes my new car for another year."

"Well, you'll want to look your very best – right down to your underwear!"

"Stop, will ye," Loughran said, but she was laughing too.

"If ye like I'll come shopping with you. And I hope you've been practicing catching the bridal bouquet too. Some of these young cops need a very broad hint."

"Jesus, Maureen, you're incorrigible!"

* * *

Lyons got home at around half past eight. She hadn't had much to drink, but she was feeling mellow after the chat with Sinéad. At half past ten, when she had finished watching the news, she went to bed. Mick wasn't in yet, but that didn't surprise her one bit. When a group of seafaring men get together for a night out, it rarely finishes early, and she didn't begrudge him his fun – he got little enough proper relaxation with the pressure of his job.

Lyons was just tucking into a plate of scrambled egg and bacon on toast at breakfast the following morning when Hays appeared.

"Coffee. I need coffee, and two paracetamol, and it's urgent!" he said, his hair all awry, in his dressing gown and slippers.

Lyons got up to attend to his needs, and he sat at the table with his head in his hands.

"Good night, then?" she said.

"Oh, don't remind me. They're a great bunch of lads, but they never know when to stop, and it would have been rude to pull out early. What did you get up to?" he said, his voice a good deal more gravelly than usual.

"I went for a meal with Sinéad at the bistro. It was fine. And guess what – she's only got a date with Peadar Tobin. His brother is getting married, and he's asked her to go."

"What, Peadar's brother?"

"No, silly, Peadar has asked Sinéad to go as his plus one," she said putting down a mug of strong coffee and two fizzing tablets in a tumbler of cold water in front of him.

"Nice. Another blossoming romance in the Gardaí. All we need now is for Pascal Brosnan and Mary Fallon to get together and we'd have a full set," Hays said.

"Careful what you wish for, hun. I think that train may have already left the station."

"Are you serious? God, sometimes I think it's a marriage bureau we're running, not a police force."

"I hope you're not complaining, Superintendent."

Hays slipped his arm around Lyons' waist and drew her close, intending to give her a reassuring kiss.

"Eww, stinky breath. Get off!"

"Oops. sorry!"

"Did you get any information from the lifeboatman about why Terry Halpin might have been out in a boat, by the way?"

"Oh, yes, I forgot. He told me that Halpin's father owns a boat. It's a cuddy boat that he uses for a bit of fishing, and he's been known to take a few tourists out around the bay in it, even though he hasn't a license. He keeps it down at Glynsk Pier, seemingly."

"Interesting. Does this boat have a name, or a number?"

"Probably, but I've no idea what it is. Why, is that relevant?"

"Could be. Leave it with me, oh, and thanks."

"At your service" – Hays gave a mock bow – "now, when do I get my morning kiss?"

"When you've brushed your teeth and shaved – if you're lucky. But you'd better be quick, I need to get to work."

Chapter Thirty

When Lyons got to the office, she had no sooner sat down at her desk, when the phone rang.

"Hello, Inspector, it's Betty here from upstairs."

"Oh, hello Betty. If you're looking for Superintendent Hays, he'll be here shortly. I left him at home, but he won't be long."

"That's OK, Inspector, it's just that we've had an Inspector Poulis from Malta on the phone looking for the superintendent. I'll have to call him back and explain."

"I'll give him a call if you like. I know what it's about," Lyons said.

"Would you? That would be great, thanks," and she read out the Maltese number for Lyons, who took it down.

"No bother, and I'll let you know if Poulis still wants Mick to call him."

"Thanks, Inspector."

Lyons looked up the international dialling code for Malta and called Inspector Poulis. It answered on the second ring.

"Poulis."

"Good morning, Inspector. My name is Inspector Maureen Lyons from Galway. I work with Superintendent

Mick Hays, and he got a message to call you. He's not in the office this morning. Is there anything I can help you with?"

"Hi, Inspector. Call me Kristoff. I wanted to have a word with Mick about the McGuires and the Halpin case that he's working on. Do you know anything about it?"

"Yes, in fact I'm the SIO on that case, so if there's anything you can tell me, or if I can help in any way, I'm at your disposal."

"Mick asked me to have a look around at Senan McGuire's brother's operation here and see what I could find. Then I got an email from him mentioning a Terry Halpin. It's interesting, because I did a search on that name, and something did come up," Poulis said.

"Excellent. What did you find out?"

"Terry Halpin was here in Malta earlier this year. He was actually staying with Ardal McGuire for a few days. Well, apparently one night they were out at the casino over at the Dragonara Hotel, and some kind of altercation broke out. The police were called. The hotel hates any of this kind of thing going on, so they tend to come down really hard on it. It was handled by our uniformed people, but I got speaking to the officer who attended the incident. It seems Halpin had had a few too many drinks and got in tow with a girl. They were getting on well, and Halpin and the girl were leaving the place when the girl's boyfriend came on the scene. He had other ideas, and the two men got into a scrap. It was quite physical, but the security guards at the casino separated the two of them, and when we arrived it was clear that Halpin was drunk, so we took him into the police station and put him in a cell for the night to sober up."

"I see. Was he charged?"

"No. We decided to let him off with a caution. We have enough to be doing here without getting involved with drunken tourists. But the security guys at the hotel told us that the boyfriend was a nasty piece of work, and he issued some fairly direct threats against Halpin."

"Did you take him in too?"

"No. We only had one car available, and we couldn't very well put them both in the back of the same vehicle, so we gave him a talking to and let him go."

"Right. Well, that's very helpful, Kristoff. Thanks for passing it on. By the way, what was the other guy called?"

"Elias Spiteri."

"OK, cool. Thanks. Is there anything else?"

"Yes, there is. It's just a local matter, but I'm placing an Impediment of Departure on Ardal McGuire. That's an instrument we use here in Malta to prevent people leaving the island if we think they have undischarged debt here. If he tries to leave, he will be stopped at the airport or the harbour. I'm hoping that Superintendent Hays will be able to help us get some evidence of whatever he's up to."

"OK. I'll pass that on to Mick and I'm sure he will be in touch. Thanks very much, Kristoff. We will talk again."

* * *

When Lyons had finished talking to the Maltese officer, she put on her jacket and collected Sally Fahy from the open plan.

"C'mon, Sally. We're off to the seaside. Bring your bucket and spade," she said jokingly.

"Right, boss. I'll just leave a note for Inspector Flynn to say where we've gone. Where are we off to by the way?"

"Glynsk harbour. It should be nice out there today, and I could do with some fresh air."

Lyons set out along the now well-trodden N59 in the direction of Clifden. As she drove along, the two detectives fell into conversation about the case.

"I heard you talking to the policeman from Malta. Was he any help, boss?" Fahy said.

"I'm not sure. Maybe. You know Terry Halpin had been out there a couple of times. Apparently, he got into some kind of a fight with one of the locals. Could be something and nothing though. He gave me the name of the other fella – an Elias someone or other. I can't remember these funny names. Have you ever been to Malta, Sally?"

"Me? No, fat chance. I've never been further than the Cork Riviera. I'm waiting for some hunky fella to sweep me off my feet and take me to the Caribbean for a nice long holiday."

"Hmm... I hear Malta is quite nice for holidays."

"Have you any holiday plans?" Fahy asked.

"No, nothing definite anyway. Mick is talking about going away in the autumn, but he's mad busy. There's yet another re-organisation on its way apparently. You remember that they were supposed to be setting up a branch of the Serious and Organised Crime Unit here. It was put on hold at the end of last year due to the election and some funding issue, but it's back on the agenda now. It's all hush-hush, but it will mean some pretty big changes for us all, I think. On the subject of which, have you thought about going for inspector at all?" Lyons said.

"No. I don't think I'm ready for it, and anyway, if I got it – and that's not a given by any means – I'd have to move to another division. There's no room for another inspector on our team unless Eamon moves on, and I don't think that's likely, do you?"

"In this game, Sally, you never know what's around the corner."

"Is there something that you're not telling me, boss?" Fahy said.

"Look, I can't go into any detail. But there are changes coming, and the more stripes you have, the better it will be for you. So, don't say anything back at the nick, but if I were you I'd start looking at the books at least."

"OK, I trust you. But not a word to anyone, OK?"

"Yes, OK and same goes for you."

* * *

When they had passed Recess and Glendollagh Lough on their left-hand side, Lyons took the next left turn onto the R340 to bring them down to Glynsk harbour. The road was narrow, so Lyons had to drive slowly, but as the scenery was quite stunning, she didn't mind a bit. As they approached their destination they passed a few abandoned and rotten boats lying in the grass, including a currach which had definitely seen better days. The currach was a very old design that originally used canvas and pitch on the hull, and had a raised bow to allow it to take on quite rough seas. But this one was retired, its canvas torn and its ribs exposed, lying at a precarious angle, slowly decaying into the ground.

Glynsk Harbour was nothing more than a small inlet where a pier and some hard standing had been constructed to allow a few fishermen to tie up their boats and unload their cargo of lobster and crab. There was a lot of debris scattered around: old bits of rope and nets and several lobster pots that were no longer in use; and the abiding smell was one of the sea and rotting fish that had been discarded here and there.

There were a total of three cuddy boats tied up alongside the little pier, and *Mary Ann* was the furthest from the harbour wall. This was apparently Halpin's vessel, and it looked to be in quite rough condition at first glance.

Lyons and Fahy parked and got out. There was an old guy in dirty clothes messing around with some bits of fishing tackle near the slipway, and Lyons strolled over to him.

"Good morning. Can you tell me, is that Hugh Halpin's boat there on the outside?" she said, nodding toward the *Mary Ann*.

"Tis all right. That's Hughie's. Why, do you want to buy her?" the old guy said with an ironic smile, revealing several missing teeth.

"Nah, you're grand. We just need to go on board for a minute or two. Do you think that would be OK?"

"Sure, it would. But be careful now – we wouldn't want you slipping into the sea in your fine smart clothes, would we?"

"We'll be fine, thanks."

The tide was about halfway in, or out, Lyons didn't know which, so it took a bit of scrambling down onto the first boat, and then a shaky transfer across the middle one till they finally set foot on *Mary Ann*. The boat was made of fibreglass, and despite initial appearances, seemed to be in better condition than they had first concluded. It had an inboard engine, with the controls located in the wheelhouse. Beside the steering position, a hatch led down into a small cabin, with benches along each side formed by the moulded fibreglass and covered in vinyl cushions. There was a marine radio in the cockpit too, and Lyons felt that the boat was pretty well equipped for what it was.

Fahy was taking a close look at the open stern section, and suddenly looked up and called to Lyons, "Boss, here, take a look at this."

Fahy had moved a couple of the plastic fish boxes away from the hull and behind where they had been stacked, she pointed to what was clearly a dried blood stain.

"Hmm. OK. It could just be fish blood," Lyons said.

"I'm not sure. Do you think we should get Sinéad out to take a sample?"

"Yeah, maybe you're right. If it is evidence, then we better not mess with it. I'll give her a call."

Chapter Thirty-one

Eamon Flynn had been busy. After a lengthy discussion with colleagues in Dublin, during which he had emailed some documents to them, he had gone in search of Superintendent Mick Hays. They had a short discussion and Hays brought him along to see Chief Superintendent Finbarr Plunkett where Flynn once again set out his case.

"Looks solid enough to me, Eamon. What do you think, Mick?" Plunkett said.

"I agree, sir."

"What do the Dublin lads say?" Plunkett said.

"They're happy we have enough, but cautioned that he will be lawyered up within minutes and we'd better have our ducks in a row because these fellas are notoriously slippery," Flynn said.

"Ah, I'd say go for it, Eamon. If nothing else we'll scare him off for a bit. But I'd hope we'd get a bit more than that," Plunkett said.

Flynn produced the warrant he had prepared earlier, and Plunkett signed it off, making a copy on his small three-in-one printer for his assistant to file away later. Betty was really a secretary, but the Gardaí had determined that this could be construed as a sexist title, so it had been replaced by 'assistant' even though there was a long tradition of male secretaries throughout the civil service.

Flynn drove around to McGuire's office in a marked squad car, accompanied by three uniformed officers. He was admitted to McGuire's premises immediately, and once inside found the man in person looking perplexed in the main reception area. He had seen the arrival through the window that looked out onto the street.

Flynn wasted no time.

"Mr McGuire, I am arresting you on suspicion of money laundering." He read him the spiel that was intended to protect the man's interests. "I have a warrant here to search these premises and take any items that we believe to be relevant to our investigations, and I need your mobile phone too please," Flynn said, waving the paper in front of McGuire who seemed disinterested in its content.

McGuire turned to Fionnula and said, "Fionnula, will you call Mr Mulvaney and tell him to meet me at the Garda station. Tell him it's important."

"Yes, of course sir, right away."

As McGuire was led away, Flynn could hear the girl on the phone to the solicitor's office making the arrangements.

Flynn left the uniformed Gardaí to bag up the stuff from McGuire's business premises. The computers would be sealed and sent under Garda escort directly to Harcourt Street in Dublin where the Gardaí kept their team of forensic accountants. They were largely consultants from some of the city's largest firms of accountants, but the Gardaí were training their own people up too, so that they would have dedicated resources to deal with the ever-growing issue of hot money circulating in the economy. In this instance, officers from the Criminal Assets Bureau would join the team investigating McGuire. This group, known as the CAB, had been very successful since its foundation in collecting cash and other assets believed to be the proceeds of crime in the state.

* * *

When McGuire had been delivered to Mill Street, he was joined by Edward Mulvaney. Mulvaney was known to the Gardaí. He seemed to turn up quite frequently when criminals were being questioned, and although he looked young and quite innocent, he could be a sharp adversary when it came to defending his clients' interests.

Flynn made himself comfortable sitting opposite Mulvaney and McGuire. He recited the usual introduction for the tape recorder, and then got started.

"Mr McGuire, we have been investigating your business activities here in the city and have a number of questions we'd like to put to you. Firstly, can you explain how an empty shop on Eyre Street that has been boarded up for years is attracting a rental income of more than €4,000 a month?"

McGuire looked at Mulvaney who shook his head slightly from side to side.

"No comment," McGuire replied.

"Well, you have to admit that it's a bit irregular. After all, who would pay such a high rent for a premises that is clearly unusable and just leave it fallow?" Flynn said.

"No comment."

"Do you own a property on Market Street, Mr McGuire?"

"Yes, I do."

"And was the upper floor of this property occupied by Terry Halpin and Keith Gillespie?"

McGuire looked for guidance to Mulvaney again. This time the solicitor nodded almost imperceptibly.

"Yes. They were working on the property, and I let them stay there while the refurbishment was going on."

"Were you aware that there was quite a large sum of money hidden in the flat?"

This time McGuire did not refer to Mulvaney before answering.

"No, of course not. If there was, it was nothing to do with me."

"What is your connection to Malta, Mr McGuire?"

"I have a brother who lives there, that's all."

"Do you visit him often?"

"Occasionally."

"Do you have any business dealings with him?"

"No. He's just family."

"Can you explain, Mr McGuire, why several large payments to alleged sub-contractors that you employ are going to non-existent companies?"

At this, Mulvaney became somewhat animated, but McGuire ignored him.

"That's nonsense. Why would I pay out money to companies that don't exist?"

"Why, indeed. But I can assure you, it's true. We have checked very carefully."

At this, Mulvaney intervened.

"My client has answered your question, Inspector. He knows nothing about any such thing. Now can we move on?"

The remainder of the interview continued in the same vein, with lots of 'no comment' when awkward questions arose. After an hour, Flynn brought matters to a halt and excused himself.

Flynn went back up to the open plan office and spoke to John O'Connor.

"Hi, John. Any idea where Inspector Lyons is?"

"She's out at Glynsk, sir. Herself and Sally Fahy have gone to examine Hugh Halpin's boat. They should be back soon. How are you getting on?"

"I'm not. I was hoping to talk to Inspector Lyons about McGuire. I have him downstairs, and it's not going well."

"Never mind, sir, maybe the forensic folks will find something."

"I hope so. I'd hate to have to release him."

* * *

Sinéad Loughran arrived out to Glynsk Pier forty minutes after she had received the call from Lyons.

"God, Maureen, you bring me to all the best places. I just love the stink of rotten fish!"

"Hi, Sinéad. I was hoping you'd have a look at this for us," Lyons said, leading Loughran over to the quay wall.

"You'll have to step down onto the first boat and then climb over – sorry!"

"That's OK. But if I fall in, don't rescue me. Send for the lifeboat – I want to be pulled out by a nice hunky crew member!"

Loughran made her way gingerly across to Halpin's little boat, and started to examine the smear of blood that had stuck to the inside of the hull and had been hidden by the empty fish boxes.

"Hmm... it's definitely blood OK, but it could be from a fish. I won't know till I get it back into town," she said, scraping some of the dark reddish-brown substance into a small plastic evidence bag.

"I think there might be a few shoe prints on the deck too. There's quite a bit of oil and grease about. Can you get anything from those?" Lyons asked.

"I'll take some pictures and see what we can do. Anything else?" Loughran said.

"There's a pair of workman's gloves in the wheelhouse by the depth finder too. There might be something useful in those."

"OK. I'll grab them too. Then, can you give me a hand to get off this thing before I get seasick?"

"Yeah, sure. C'mon," Lyons said, leading her colleague carefully across the other two boats and safely back onto the harbour wall.

"Thanks. I'll get these back to town and call you later when I've had a look. Oh, by the way, I was having another look at that shoe we got from your friend in the van. Right at the heel, on the inside, nearly worn away there were two initials. It looks like FS, or maybe ES, but they are a bit indistinct. Don't know if that's any use?" Loughran said.

"Ah, Elias Spiteri perchance?" Fahy said.

Chapter Thirty-two

Lyons was heading up the evening briefing at five o'clock when she got back to the station.

"OK, folks, settle down. Let's see what we've got. Eamon, you go first."

"Thanks, boss. Well we have McGuire in custody. I've spoken to Plunkett and he's happy that we have enough to charge him with money laundering, and I'm hoping we can have him remanded while the forensic people go through the stuff we took from his office."

"Excellent. Out of courtesy, it might be a good ideal to let Poulis know," Lyons said.

"You mean McGuire's brother will find out, and that might spook them into some kind of unplanned action," Flynn said.

"You know me too well, Eamon. Exactly! And there's more. Sally and I were out at Glynsk earlier and we found blood smears on Hugh Halpin's boat. Sinéad Loughran is analysing them right now to see if they match anyone we know, although in fairness, it could just be fish guts."

A ripple of laughter went around the room.

"She also found the initials ES or FS inside the shoe that we recovered from the burnt remains in the van at

Loch Bollard, and we think the guy that died may have been an Elias Spiteri – a Maltese national. Eamon, when you're speaking to Poulis will you ask him about that? Ask him to check with the shoe shop to see if one such purchased a pair, if he doesn't suggest it himself. They might even scout around and see if Spiteri is at home too," Lyons said.

"Yes, sure."

"Oh, there's something else. We got the analysis back from Terry Halpin's phone that Gillespie gave us – well, sort of gave us, anyway. There's nothing incriminating on it, but there's quite a few calls between himself and his father in the days before he was killed. But I don't know if that's significant. Gillespie said he thought Terry had another phone, but we haven't found that. OK, let's leave it at that for today. Eamon, you keep going with McGuire. Let's get him before a judge and see if we can get him remanded as a flight risk. I think it might be worth having another chat with Hugh Halpin, but we'll wait to see what Sinéad has to say about the stuff we found on his boat. That's all then. Goodnight, everyone," Lyons said.

Lyons went back to her office as the team dispersed. When she was alone, she sat down and consulted her notebook. She took out a burner mobile that she had in a drawer and dialled the number Sally Fahy had given her for Cónan O'Neill. It was answered on the second ring, and it was clear that the man was driving, but had the phone connected to a hands-free system.

"Hi, is that Cónan?" she said, trying to sound younger and more innocent.

"Yes, who's this?"

"My name is Maureen, Cónan. I wonder if you can help me?"

"What's on your mind, love?"

"I got your name from someone. You see, my sister is getting married in a few weeks and we need to buy a lot of drink in. Can you help with that?"

"Maybe, but won't the hotel be supplying all the drink for the guests?"

"Oh, no. We're having the reception at home. Dad has hired a big tent thing."

"Oh right. So how many are coming then?"

"I think it's about seventy or eighty altogether, but do you think you could get us some spirits and wines at a good price?" Lyons said.

"Yes, sure, no bother. How much do you want?"

"Let's see. I made a list here somewhere. Yes, here it is. We need a case each of gin, vodka and whiskey and about ten cases of wine – half red and half white. This needs to be good stuff though, none of yer plonk. Oh and some mixers. What would all that cost?"

"Hang on. I'll just pull over and do a few calculations."

Lyons could hear O'Neill's van going down through the gears and coming to a halt. A few moments later, he was back on the line.

"Let's see now, love, I make it just over €720 – let's say €700 even, but I don't do mixers, but you can get them cheaply enough at Tesco. When do you need it?"

"As soon as you like. But I don't want you coming to the house. Let's meet somewhere convenient when you have it ready."

"OK. And that's cash, by the way."

"Yes, of course, that's not a problem."

"Look, I'll have this together tomorrow. Why don't we meet out at the Udarás car park at Furbo tomorrow at, say, ten o'clock. It's very quiet there. I'll be in a blue van. Does that suit?"

"Yes, OK, I'll find it. Ten o'clock you say?"

"Yes, ten, oh and you can come on your own, I'll lift the boxes into your car for you."

"Thanks, Cónan. See you there."

Although she had told O'Neill that she would meet him on her own, she had no intention of doing so. She decided to take Sally with her. She could pass her off as her sister, and she believed that another girl wouldn't frighten the man away. His desire to get his hands on the cash would outweigh his misgivings.

She just caught Fahy before she left the office and outlined the plan.

"You're firearms trained, Sally, aren't you?"

"Yes, sure, boss. Do you want me to tool up?"

"Might be best. This dude is from the North after all, so he may be armed, and he definitely won't want to get arrested."

"OK. I'll draw a weapon tomorrow, early doors. What time do you want to leave here?" Fahy said.

"Let's meet here at eight for a briefing before we go out to Furbo. It's only about half an hour in the car, so we can leave at nine-twenty or so, get there before O'Neill. OK?"

"Yes, that's fine. See you tomorrow. Oh, by the way, Sinéad was looking for you when you were on the phone. She asked if you could call her back," Fahy said.

"Thanks, I'll give her a call now."

* * *

"Hi, Sinéad. You were looking for me," Lyons said when she got through to the forensic lab.

"Oh, hi Maureen, yes, thanks for calling back. I did some work on the blood we found out on Halpin's boat. I can't be totally certain, but I'd say there's a good chance that it belongs to Terry Halpin. I'm sending it off for DNA testing to make sure."

"Hmm... OK. How sure are you?"

"Seventy-five percent. It's the same blood group, but we need the DNA analysis to be certain. I've asked for it to be expedited, so we could know tomorrow or the next day."

"OK, thanks. Let me know as soon as you have anything."

"'course."

Chapter Thirty-three

Lyons and Fahy met at the station early the following morning. They were both dressed similarly, and despite the age gap, they could easily have been taken for sisters although Fahy was blonde, while Lyons had dark chestnut hair.

Sally Fahy wore a bulky, padded jacket, ideal for concealing the side arm that she had checked out of the armoury first thing.

"I hate these things. I hope to God I don't have to use it. Do you really think O'Neill will be armed? He thinks he's just meeting one ditsy girl after all," Fahy said.

"Thanks, Sally! Best not to take any chances in any case. If I'm going to get shot at again, I want to be able to fire back! No more Miss Nice Guy!"

"OK. Are we all set?"

"Yep! Let's do it."

They took Lyons' dark-coloured Volvo and drove out along the coast road, through Salthill, on past Barna and finally into Furbo. O'Neill had been right – the large car park that surrounded the Udarás building was almost deserted, and they parked up where they could observe the arrival of any vehicles. Ten o'clock came and went, with no sign of O'Neill.

At ten past, Lyons was about to call him again on the burner phone she had used the previous day, when a dirty and rather bashed up dark blue Ford Transit pulled into the car park. O'Neill turned the van and reversed up alongside the Volvo so that the rear doors were adjacent to the boot of Lyons' car. They all got out.

"Hi, I'm Maureen and this is my sister, Sally," Lyons said introducing them. O'Neill made no remark about there being two of them. He was just keen to get on with the transaction and get out of there.

"Money. I need your money first," he said, rather gruffly.

Lyons pulled the roll of notes she had acquired the previous evening from the desk sergeant at Mill Street when she had completed the necessary forms and had the cash signed off by Hays. O'Neill reached out to take the money.

"Hold on," Lyons said, "let me see the drinks."

O'Neill stared at the two detectives for a moment without saying anything.

"Not just a pretty face, are you?" he said, and turned to open the back doors of the van. Inside, Lyons and Fahy could see cardboard boxes with the names of various well-known spirit manufacturers printed on them.

O'Neill reached in, opened the nearest box, and produced a bottle of Gordon's gin. Lyons noticed that it was in a green bottle. In other words, it had been intended for the UK home market. She knew well enough that the Gordon's sold in Ireland was in a clear bottle and was in fact stronger than the domestic product.

"Is that the real thing?" she asked. "Dad has some Gordon's at home and it's in a different bottle."

"It sure is. Do you want to taste it?"

"No, it's OK thanks. I hate gin," she said, handing over the money.

Fahy went to the back of Lyons' car and opened the boot.

O'Neill reached into the van and lifted one of the boxes, carrying it around to the back of Lyons' car and putting it in the boot. He repeated this with another box. When he was carrying the third box of spirits from the van, Lyons blocked his way, and holding up her warrant card, started to recite the arrest mantra.

O'Neill was quick. He threw the box at Lyons, knocking her over, hopped into the back of his van pulling the doors closed behind him, and before the detectives could sort themselves out, he had scrambled into the driver's seat, started the Transit and was driving out of the car park at high speed.

"Shit! C'mon. Let's get after him!" Lyons said, jumping into her own car and setting off in pursuit.

"Get on the radio, Sally. Get them to put roadblocks up at Moycullen on both the Galway and the Clifden sides of the crossroads – that's where this comes out, if he doesn't double back on us."

Lyons gunned the Volvo, and it wasn't long before they saw the back of the Transit hurtling along at high speed, bouncing wildly on the uneven, boggy road.

O'Neill must have seen them approaching in his rear-view mirror, because he suddenly swerved onto a really narrow boreen that Lyons knew led up past some holiday cottages, before re-joining the L1320 that would take him into Moycullen.

"Damn! There's no chance of passing him on this road. Let's just stay behind him. We might get a chance to nab him when it widens out further on," Lyons said.

But they needn't have worried. O'Neill misjudged one of the bends on the narrow road. The van hit the ditch, and the old Transit rose up on two wheels before turning over and skidding along on its side in a shower of smoke and sparks. The back doors flew open, and bottles and boxes spilled out and smashed on the stony surface.

Before Lyons had stopped the car completely, Fahy was out the door, drawing her weapon as she ran towards the stricken vehicle. She went to the front of it where the windscreen had been blown out in the smash, and pointed her weapon at Cónan O'Neill who was conscious and bleeding from the face, but otherwise seemed to be more or less intact.

"As my colleague was saying, I'm arresting you on suspicion of smuggling alcohol into the state for the purpose of avoiding excise duty." She continued with the rest of the recitation as required by the procedure.

* * *

It took over two hours to sort out the mess. Most of the booze from the van had been lost in the crash, but there was enough in the boot of Lyons' car to provide evidence of O'Neill's crime. A tow truck was sent out from Galway to retrieve the van – an awkward manoeuvre given the narrowness of the road, but it was eventually loaded onto the back of the recovery vehicle and taken back to Mill Street.

An ambulance had arrived to take O'Neill off to hospital, and Sally Fahy accompanied him to make sure that he didn't attempt an escape, though in fairness, given his condition, she thought that was unlikely.

Lyons waited till all the other vehicles had been taken away. She borrowed a sweeping brush from a woman in one of the holiday cottages who was amazed at the drama that had unfolded in this normally very quiet rural idyll, and cleared the road of broken glass. One bottle of chardonnay had somehow remained in one piece, and Lyons retrieved it from the long grass at the side of the road and put it in the cubby between the seats in her car. It was mid-afternoon by the time she got back to Mill Street to find that Sally Fahy was already there ahead of her.

"How's your man?" Lyons said.

"Ah, he's grand. A bit grumpy, but no real harm done to him. I handed him over to the uniformed lads to look after him. The van is stolen, of course, no surprises there. And we should be able to trace the source of his supply from the serial numbers stamped on the reverse side of the labels on the spirits. There are a good few bottles still undamaged," Fahy said.

"Have you handed in your weapon?"

"I have. Glad to get rid of it to be honest. Anyway, are you OK?"

"Oh, yeah, fine. I borrowed a brush and cleared the road of glass before I left. That's what kept me. When do you think we'll get to interview O'Neill?"

"Tomorrow, I'd say. Why, what do you want from him, apart from the obvious?" Fahy said.

"A list of his customers. Then we'll hand that on upstairs. I'm not getting into a scrap with loads of publicans in the area. I'd never get a drink again!" Lyons said, and they both laughed.

"I'd better let Séan Mulholland know that we have O'Neill in custody. God knows how many small pubs out his way have been buying from him."

Chapter Thirty-four

As Lyons and Fahy were finishing up the saga of the smuggled alcohol, Eamon Flynn came back into the office.

"Hi, Eamon, how did it go?" Lyons asked.

"He wasn't remanded. But he has to surrender his passport and report to us every three days till the trial. There's plenty of evidence to get him for money laundering anyway. The forensic accountants say he's not nearly as clever as he thinks he is. He's left trails all over the place. How did you get on?"

"Ah, ye know, just a pleasant drive in the country snagging a smuggler who crashed his van and spilt good whiskey all over the road. Nothing out of the ordinary!" Lyons said, and Fahy giggled.

"God, Maureen, you don't do things by halves, do you?" Flynn said.

"Right. But we still aren't any nearer to solving these two murders. Do you think there's a link to McGuire's activity and the death of the two lads, Eamon?"

"There's definitely some connection, but I don't think McGuire killed either of them. He's too much of a desk jockey for that kind of activity. But he may well be mixed up in it in some way. Do you want me to bring him back in?"

"No, not yet in any case. Let's see what the fraud squad uncover about his money laundering. But what I don't get is why the Maltese guy was here in the first place," Lyons said.

"Maybe they carry some of the hot money from Malta in cash. You know, as couriers," Fahy said.

"I doubt it. Too risky. It's much easier to move it electronically these days."

Lyons went to her office, and Eamon Flynn followed her in and sat down in front of her desk.

"Any thoughts?" he said.

"Give me a few minutes to cool down after that business out at Furbo. What about you? Have you any ideas?"

"Nothing definite. Just a feeling about Halpin's father. I got the impression he wasn't being entirely up front with us. Did you sense that too?" Flynn said.

"I can't say I did, but you could be right. Let's see if Sinéad can get a match on the blood found on his boat and then we could go and have another chat with him. What do you say?"

"Yes. Good idea. When will she know?"

"Later today, or tomorrow, I think."

* * *

True to her word, Sinéad Loughran called Lyons at just after half past four.

"Hi, Sinéad, what's up?" Lyons said.

"Hi, Maureen. It's about that blood from Hugh Halpin's boat. It's Terry's all right – no doubt."

"I see. But there wasn't that much of it, was there. He might have just cut himself at some stage when he was out with his dad."

"True. Would you like us to go back to the boat and give it a really thorough going over? It might have more to tell us."

"Let's leave it for now. It's not going anywhere, after all. We can get to it later if we need to."

"No problem," Sinéad said.

Lyons spent the rest of the afternoon completing the paperwork surrounding the arrest of Cónan O'Neill – a not insubstantial task in its own right. She sent John O'Connor down to her car to remove the bootleg drink and store it in the evidence room, and when he was finished he brought her keys back to her in her office.

"Nice little haul for the Christmas party you got there, boss," he said.

"Now, now, John. You know all that has to go to auction when the case is over. But it does look like good hooch all the same. Let's see what happens."

The rest of the day slipped by quickly, and before Lyons knew it, it was after six. When she realised the time, she rang Mick Hays on her mobile.

"Hi, Mick. Where are you?"

"I'm at home slaving over a hot stove. What about you?"

"Oh, nice. Something tasty I hope, I'm starving."

"Better get your ass back here then pronto before it spoils. Are you still at the office?"

"Yep, just leaving. I have a nice bottle of wine for us to have with our dinner too!"

"Excellent. See you in a few minutes then."

* * *

When they had finished the really excellent meal that Hays had prepared, and drunk the entire bottle of wine that Lyons had taken from the crash scene, Hays asked her, "What's the story about our property deal? I have the money all set up now, and the surveyor got back to me. It's in pretty good condition, or so he says."

"Oh, yes, sorry, I meant to say. It's all systems go. As soon as we can get five minutes to spare, we should have a meeting with the solicitor and hand over the cash. Then he'll get on and register the conveyance, and hey presto – job done."

"It all seems so easy, doesn't it. But you should be careful to keep an account of where the money came from. If we ever come under scrutiny, we need to be able to demonstrate that it's fully legit," Hays said.

"That's not a problem. Sheila's accountant has prepared proper documentation about the money she's giving me, and the rest is savings that have built up gradually over the years. I've been putting part of my salary away each month, and the bank records will reflect that. What about your share?" Lyons said.

"I got most of it in brown envelopes from various criminals for services rendered," Hays said, watching his partner going pale and her eyes flaring.

"Joke! Honestly, Maureen, you should see your face! Most of mine is inheritance from my parents. It's all well documented and the taxes were paid at the time, so it's all on record."

"Has this cleaned you out?"

"No, not at all, and in any case it's a good idea. Lots of our colleagues are invested in property in one way or another. I reckon it's a sound long-term proposition."

"Let's hope so. We're getting it at a very good price anyway, so if we run out of cash, we should be able to flip it easily enough. But I'd rather hold on to it if possible. My father always said a steady income is the key to prosperity."

"A wise man, your father," Hays said.

Chapter Thirty-five

Lyons was holding court the following morning with Sally Fahy, Eamon Flynn and John O'Connor all seated around her in the open plan.

"Right, tasks for the day. Eamon, have you anything more to do with Senan McGuire?"

"No, boss. I've written it all up. I've handed it over to the specialists now. I'll need to go to court eventually and give evidence of his arrest and caution, but that won't be for months."

"Great, I'd like you to go out and talk to Hugh Halpin again then. See if he can give you an explanation for his son's blood in the boat. Don't be too easy on him. I know he's bereaved, but he's no shrinking violet, so see if you can rattle him a bit."

"Shall I bring him in for questioning, boss?"

"See what you think. If he's acting shifty, then yes, definitely."

"OK. I'm on it," Flynn said.

"Sally, I want you to liaise with Customs and Excise. Give them the full story of what Cónan O'Neill has been up to. He probably has a place where he stores all that smuggled booze too. They need to find that and close him down."

"Right, I'll get onto them as soon as we're finished here. Are we going to charge him with anything ourselves?"

"Let's see what Customs say. I reckon he'll have his plate full without us adding to it, and what have we got anyway? Resisting arrest? Dangerous driving? Hold off till we see how it's going. I don't want too much paperwork to have to deal with, and the smuggling is much more serious."

"OK. What are you going to do, boss?" Fahy asked, as she nearly always did.

"I need to have a word with Séan Mulholland. Oh, Eamon, before you go, did you get anything more from the Maltese police?"

"Yes, thanks for reminding me. Poulis would like you to call him."

"Hmm... OK. I'll call him after I've spoken to Séan. OK, that's it for now. If anything breaks, let me know at once, won't you?"

The all replied in the affirmative and the meeting broke up.

* * *

"Hello, Séan, it's Maureen. Have you got a minute?"

"Of course, for you, Maureen, any time."

"Good. Listen I thought you should know we have the man who's been delivering smuggled liquor to Tigh Oisrí in custody. We nabbed him yesterday trying to sell me a load of hot Northern Ireland stuff. Customs and Excise are dealing with him, but if he tells them everything he's been up to, they may decide to visit some of the pubs out your way," Lyons said.

"Oh, I see what you mean. It wouldn't be good if they were to find a pile of illegal drink on the premises. That would be the end of the road for a lot of the small boozers out in the sticks, and that would go very hard on the locals."

"Just what I was thinking, Séan. Can I leave it with you?"

"Of course, Maureen, and thanks."

When Lyons had finished the call, the front desk rang her to say that a Keith Gillespie had been on looking for her, and he wanted her to call him back.

Lyons wasted no time in ringing Gillespie using Terry Halpin's number, and the man answered immediately.

"Hi, Keith. You were looking for me?"

"Hi. Yeah. Listen, can we meet? Just you and me."

"OK. What's up?"

"I'm not saying nothing on the phone. I'm in Galway. Let's say the Insomnia coffee shop on Cross Street in half an hour, OK?"

"Yes, yes OK. But it would be really helpful if you could tell me what it's about. I'm very busy today."

But the line had gone dead.

Lyons just had time to put a call in to Malta before she would have to leave the office to make the rendezvous with Gillespie. She got through to Inspector Poulis very quickly.

"Thanks for calling," the Maltese policeman said. "I just wanted to let you know that Elias Spiteri did fly to Dublin on the Tuesday, two weeks before you found his body. I think we can be certain that the identity is confirmed. I checked with the shoe shop, and they told me that he had purchased those Spanish shoes as well. The girl remembered him, because they don't sell many of that particular brand, and he chatted her up."

"I see. Well I'm sorry to say we haven't got anywhere near solving how he came to be found cremated in the bog here, but we're obviously still working on it. I'll let you know if we get any kind of breakthrough. By the way, what did Spiteri work at?"

"That's the interesting thing, Inspector. He was employed by Ardal McGuire as a handyman, or so they told us when we contacted McGuire's office. They said he's just disappeared. They couldn't give us any more information, I'm afraid."

"OK. Well thanks a lot for that, Inspector. You should know that we have Ardal McGuire's brother in custody here for money laundering. When we get enough evidence to implicate the brother, I'll send it over to you. Is Ardal still around?"

"Oh yes. He won't find it easy to slip away, believe me."

"Excellent. Thanks again. We'll be in touch. Bye."

* * *

Lyons got her jacket from the back of her chair and left the office to walk around to Cross Street. She didn't tell any of the others where she was off to, or who she was going to meet. She reckoned she was safe enough in a busy coffee shop, and in any case Gillespie had proved to be no threat the last time they met.

It only took her ten minutes to cover the distance to the coffee shop, so she spent a little while just observing. Nothing looked amiss, so she eventually went inside and ordered a cappuccino and a hot croissant, and sat down at a quiet table near the back. She had just finished the snack when she saw Gillespie entering the premises looking furtive, dressed in dirty jeans and a grey hoodie. He spotted her immediately and sat down at her table.

"Hello, Keith. Can I get you a coffee, or a tea?" Lyons said.

"No thanks. I don't want to be seen in here with you, but I do need a word."

"OK. What's up?"

"Look, I think I'm being followed, and I've received a few threats too. I'm scared."

"So, what do you want me to do about it?"

"I need to get away, but I'm skint. I need some folding – and fast!"

"What do I get if I help you, Keith?"

"Information."

"OK, off you go, and I'll see what I can do."

"How much can you give me?"

"That depends on what you have for me. A few hundred if it all checks out, and gets us somewhere."

"Right. Well, listen. I know a good bit more about what Terry was up to than I said. He was mixed up with this Maltese crowd big time. You know he'd been out there?" Gillespie said.

"Yes, we knew that. But what exactly was he up to?"

"He was helping McGuire to funnel the hot money through his businesses here, and he was acting as a courier too from time to time. Last time he was down there, he brought back a hundred grand in cash. He had a suitcase with a false compartment, and no one suspected him."

"I see. And are you prepared to testify to this effect, Keith?"

"Not likely! That McGuire fella has some very nasty friends. It would be more than my life is worth!"

"Well that's hardly worth a few hundred euros. We can't exactly prosecute Terry Halpin, now can we?" Lyons said.

"There's more."

"Go on."

"Halpin killed the young Maltese guy. Yer man, Spiteri I think his name was, was one of the couriers and he was bringing a pile of cash up here. But when Terry had been in Malta, he had stolen Spiteri's girl, and when he turned up here, they got into a fight. Terry hit him with some of our builders' stuff, and yer man's head just caved in – or so he told me."

"How did Spiteri end up in a burnt-out van, Keith?"

"I dunno. Someone helped Terry. They hid the body for a while, and then I guess it was starting to stink, so he was put in the van and set on fire."

"And who was the someone in question?"

"Search me."

"And do you swear that you had nothing whatever to do with any of these killings, Keith?"

"No, course not. But I know too much. Someone wants me silenced. You have to help me."

"OK. But I need you to make a proper statement. Tell you what. Meet me here again tomorrow at this time. I'll have your cash. Then get the train to Dublin. Make sure you're not followed. Go to Pearse Street Garda Station and ask for an Inspector Healy. He'll take your statement and then you can go into hiding. OK?"

"I guess. Same time tomorrow then. Right, I'm off."

Lyons barely noticed Keith Gillespie leaving the place.

"It's amazing how some of these people can virtually disappear into the crowd," she said to herself, before musing, "I hope to Christ I've done the right thing!"

Chapter Thirty-six

Eamon Flynn took Sally Fahy with him to drive out to Hugh Halpin's cottage at Screebe.

Fahy was driving fast – so much so that Flynn felt the need to comment.

"Cripes, Sally, you don't hang around, do you?"

"I've done the advanced driving test, so you're quite safe, boss. No point having a squad car if you can't have some fun in it, is there? Do you want me to slow down?"

"Nah, you're fine. We'll get there a bit quicker I guess." And with that, Fahy overtook a large white delivery van, flooring the Hyundai and maxing the engine revs up to the red line.

They pulled up at a more sedate pace outside Halpin's cottage in Screebe twenty-five minutes later.

"How do you want to play this, boss?" Fahy asked.

"Just as it comes. But I don't see Hugh's jeep anywhere. Maybe he's not here."

The half-door to the cottage was open as usual, and the smell of baking wafted out on the gentle breeze as they approached the house. Inside, they could see Halpin's wife mixing away at the kitchen table, her hands covered in flour. Flynn knocked on the doorjamb, and the woman looked up.

"Oh, 'tis yourself," she said, wiping her hands in her apron and approaching the door.

"Come on in. Have you news for us?"

"No, I'm afraid not, Mrs Halpin, though the case is progressing. Is your husband about?" Flynn said.

"No, he's gone out. He's in very bad form, officer. I don't know what's come over him. He barely speaks anymore."

"Do you know where he's gone?" Fahy said.

"No, he didn't say. If you find him, tell him to get home. I'll look after him."

The two Gardaí turned to leave the house again, and as they were opening the door, Mrs Halpin spoke up again.

"But, Inspector, he's got a gun."

Flynn turned to look at the woman.

"A shotgun?"

"No. An old revolver. His grandfather was mixed up in the Civil War, and he kept his gun. He handed it down to Hugh's father, and he passed it on to Hugh. He has ammunition for it too."

"OK, well if he comes back, please let us know at once. We'll go and see if we can find him," Flynn said, handing the woman one of his cards.

When they were back in the car, Fahy called Séan Mulholland in Clifden.

"Sergeant, it's Sally Fahy. I'm here at Hugh Halpin's cottage with Inspector Flynn. Mrs Halpin tells us that her husband has gone walkabout and he has a weapon, apparently. Will you put out a code red for him. You know the drill – may be armed, approach with extreme caution. And can you get Pascal Brosnan to meet us down at Glynsk pier. I have a feeling he may be hanging around down there."

"Right, so. God, I hope he'll not do himself harm. I'd best get on. I'll alert all the nearby stations right away."

"Thanks, Sergeant. We'll let you know if there are any developments."

With Flynn driving this time, Fahy called the situation into Maureen Lyons in Galway.

"OK, Sally, we'd best get a few uniforms around to Senan McGuire's place in case he's coming after him. Do you need me to come out?"

"No, not yet in any case. I'll let you know as soon as anything develops."

* * *

Pascal Brosnan arrived at Glynsk Pier at the same time as Flynn and Fahy. They got out of their cars, and saw at once that Hugh Halpin's boat was no longer tied up alongside the harbour wall. They all looked out to sea, and Fahy said, "There's a boat out there that could be him. Your ten o'clock, boss."

Flynn squinted in that direction and could make out a blob, but couldn't identify it.

"I have binoculars in my car, hold on, I'll go and get them," Brosnan said.

He retrieved the glasses from the glove box, and handed them to Flynn.

"It could be him, OK. It's hard to tell. Here, why don't you liberate that inflatable Avon dinghy there, Pascal, and we'll go out and see what's what."

Brosnan untied the little grey boat from its moorings. It had an outboard engine attached, so Brosnan hopped down into it, and set about starting the engine. After ten pulls on the starting cord, he spotted that the engine's kill switch was set to 'OFF'. As soon as he changed its position, the little motor burst into life in a cloud of blue exhaust smoke.

"Is there enough fuel, Pascal? The last thing we need is to get stuck out at sea."

"Yes. The tank is near full. Should be enough for a couple of hours," Brosnan said.

"Will she take the three of us?" Fahy said.

"Better with two, I'd say. Which one of you will come with me?"

"I'll go. I'm a bit lighter, and the Inspector can stay here and co-ordinate things if needs be," Fahy said, looking to her boss for approval.

"Righto. Off you go then, but be careful. Remember, if it is him, he has a weapon," Flynn said.

"We'll be fine," Fahy replied, but not feeling too sure that they would.

Brosnan navigated the little inflatable away from the pier and set off towards what they believed could be Hugh Halpin's boat, which he reckoned was some two miles out. Fortunately, the sea was calm, and the dinghy made good time, throwing up a white spray as it cut through the gentle waves.

When they were about halfway to where their target sat bobbing about, they could identify the vessel and the man on board.

Fahy used her radio to call back to Flynn.

"It's Hugh Halpin, all right, sir. He doesn't seem to be moving. We're closing on him now."

"Thanks, Sally."

As the Avon got within 30 metres or so of Halpin's boat, Hugh Halpin stood up and pointed his revolver at the Gardaí.

"Don't come any closer. I'll shoot," he roared, brandishing the weapon, although they both noticed that his hand was shaking as he did so.

"Put down the gun, Hugh. We just need to talk. Don't make matters any worse, just put down the weapon so we can approach."

"Go away. I'll shoot you know. I don't care anymore!"

"That won't bring Terry back, Hugh. Now be sensible and put down the gun. We can sort all this out."

Halpin stared at Fahy for several minutes, and then in an act of resignation, he flopped down onto the bench seat that ran between the gunwales of his fishing boat, and put his head in his hands. Flynn and Fahy could hear the revolver hitting the deck.

They approached cautiously, and when they were alongside, Fahy, being the nimbler of the two, clambered aboard Hugh Halpin's boat. She first moved the gun away down to the stern of the vessel with her foot, and then took out her handcuffs, and recited the arrest mantra to the man, who seemed to be in some sort of daze.

"What do we do now?" Brosnan called from the dinghy.

"Come aboard, and tie that thing off at the stern. Then you can drive us back to the pier while I watch Mr Halpin here."

As Brosnan did the necessary, Fahy got on the radio again.

"Inspector, we have Mr Halpin in custody. The firearm has been recovered. No shots fired. All good. We're coming back in."

"Roger, Sally. Well done. Are you both OK?"

"Just a little seasick, sir, but yes – we're fine."

Chapter Thirty-seven

The Gardaí arrived back in Mill Street with their prisoner later that morning. Halpin had said nothing at all on the journey, and just looked down at his feet the whole time, as if he were totally dejected.

Lyons had been preparing to question him, and had already alerted the duty solicitor who wasted no time in attending the station.

Lyons had stood down the code red for Hugh Halpin, and Flynn had decided to take Pascal Brosnan back out to Roundstone, stopping by Screebe on the way to give Mrs Halpin the good news that her husband was safe and well, albeit in custody. He wanted to have a look around Halpin's workshop while he was there.

Lyons took Sally Fahy with her to the interview room, where Halpin was seated alongside Eoin Lawless, the solicitor. They had no sooner sat down than Lawless started to speak.

"My client wishes to make clear that at no time did he intend to harm any of your officers, Inspector. He was just taken by surprise when they arrived alongside his boat."

"Hmm... thought we were pirates, did he? He pointed a gun at one of my officers and said he was about to shoot –

so I think we'll let a jury decide what he intended. Now, Mr Halpin, I want you to tell me all that you know about the death of your son, Terry, and his associate from Malta."

Halpin stared at Lyons for what seemed like ages, but was in fact only a minute.

"Mr Halpin?" Lyons said.

"It was an accident. I didn't mean to harm him. He just fell awkwardly on the boat," Halpin said.

Lawless touched the arm of his client and said, "I'd advise you not to say anything further, Mr Halpin."

But Hugh Halpin wanted to unburden himself, and Lawless wasn't going to stop him.

"Why don't we start at the beginning, Mr Halpin. Tell me the whole story," Lyons said, recognising Halpin's demeanour.

"It started with that Maltese fella. He was one of McGuire's couriers, and he came to Ireland to deliver cash. But Terry knew him from before – when he was in Malta. There was some trouble over a girl, and the two fell out. Anyway, they had both been drinking out at that place in Kilnatrá. McDermott threw them out, cos they were getting loud and aggressive. But outside, they got into a scuffle, and it ended with the Maltese fella falling against that iron fence McDermott has up to protect the caravans in the car park. Terry came to me in a terrible state and asked me to help him."

"Do you mean the Maltese man was actually dead?"

"Yes. Terry wrapped him up in some of that heavy plastic from the building stuff he had in the van and dragged the body inside one of the old ruined cottages down there."

"So, what happened after that?"

"I didn't see Terry for a few days. Then one evening he came out to the house. He told me the whole story. He was in an awful state. He was a nervous lad in any case – always had been. He said he'd been getting threats from

McGuire, and he was afraid McGuire would discover what he'd done and come after him. So, I suggested that we go down to the boat and do some fishing. That used to settle Terry down when he was an angry teenager. A couple of hours at sea casting a line for mackerel is worth more than all your psychotherapy put together."

"You and Terry went out in your boat then?"

"Yes, we did. We drove down to Glynsk in my car and took the boat out. But he couldn't settle. He started arguing with me. Told me it was all my fault. That if I'd been any kind of a father he would have had money and he wouldn't have had to get mixed up with all this. We both got fierce riled up. We were kind of grappling with each other. I thought we might go overboard, so I grabbed the nearest thing that came to hand, and struck him on the head. I must have hit him terrible hard, cos he slumped down immediately. It took me a few minutes to gather myself, but when I bent down to see what condition he was in, it was clear that he was dead. The light had gone from his eyes." Halpin's own eyes filled with tears.

"Clearly a case of self-defence, officer," Lawless said.

"What did you do then?" Fahy said.

"What could I do. I couldn't take him back to Glynsk. I put some weights from the lobster pots on his feet and heaved him over the side."

"But that doesn't explain how the body of the Maltese man ended up in the van, Mr Halpin."

"That was me. After Terry died, I reckoned the place down there would be swarming with you lot, and it wouldn't be long before the body was discovered. So, one night, I went down in the old van that Terry had been using, put the body in it, and drove it up to Lough Bollard. You know the rest," Halpin said.

"I see. Why didn't you come to us and report it?" Lyons said.

"He was my son. You don't grass on family!"

"I need a few minutes with Mr Halpin, Inspector. Could we take a short break?" Lawless said.

"Yes, of course. I'll arrange tea or coffee. Shall we say half an hour?"

"Yes, thank you."

Once outside the interview room, Lyons asked Fahy to get Sinéad Loughran and her team back out to Glynsk and go over the boat with a fine-tooth comb.

"We need something to corroborate his story. I've a feeling he's going to go for diminished responsibility. Get onto her, will you?"

"Yes, sure, boss."

* * *

When the interview with Hugh Halpin resumed, Eoin Lawless was the first to speak.

"Before we go any further, Inspector, I want to put in a request for my client to be assessed by a psychologist. He's obviously very disturbed – who wouldn't be after the death of their only son – and I'm not sure he's capable of giving evidence in his present state."

"Very well. But I should remind you that there are some very serious charges coming at your client. So far, we have manslaughter, aiding and abetting after the fact, and threatening a police officer with an unlicensed weapon, and I do intend to pursue these charges, regardless of Mr Halpin's mental condition," Lyons said.

"Well, that's for later, Inspector. For now, can we just make the arrangements?" Lawless said.

"Very well. We'll be keeping Mr Halpin here with us while this assessment as you call it is carried out, of course."

"Of course."

* * *

When Lawless had left, and Halpin had been returned to his cell with his own clothing having been replaced with a safety suit, in case he might attempt self-harm, Lyons instructed the desk sergeant to check on him every thirty minutes and to make sure to update the log.

She then went in search of Superintendent Hays.

"What do you think?" she said after she had told Hays the full story in his office at the top of the station.

"Hmm... Hard to say. It looks to me as if the diminished responsibility thing will probably stick. Filicide is pretty unusual, and the courts don't like it one little bit. Let's see what the report brings, and then I'll have a word with Plunkett and we'll see how to proceed. Have you told the Maltese police what has unfolded?"

"No, not yet. I hope they don't decide to send what's left of Spiteri back to Malta. That would be very brutal on the guy's family."

"That's not up to us. But I know what you mean. What about McGuire and the other eejit with the smuggled booze?"

"All in hand, Superintendent. A nice few bob for the Criminal Assets Bureau, and enough illicit hooch to float a battleship which will fetch a good price at auction," Lyons said.

"How come?"

"O'Neill gave us the location of his store. It was up near the border in Donegal. We sent the local lads in to sort it and they say they got around a hundred grand's worth of liquor. Customs are prosecuting O'Neill – I'd say he'll get a few years inside."

"And has any more of the stuff turned up on our patch?"

"Séan Mulholland is looking after that, Mick."

"Jesus! Looking after is right. Are you OK with that?"

"I am. We can't close all the boozers between Galway and Clifden. There would be riots, and in any case it wouldn't be fair. Séan is an old hand at this sort of thing. He'll sort it out, don't worry."

* * *

Later that day, Sinéad Loughran breezed into the detective suite at Mill Street clutching a plastic evidence bag and looking smug.

"What you got there?" John O'Connor said when he saw her.

"Wouldn't you like to know. Is Maureen in?"

"Yeah, she's in her office."

Loughran went to Lyons' office and knocked on the open door.

"Come in, Sinéad. Grab a seat. What have you there?"

"From Halpin's boat. It was in the bottom of some very nasty gunge in the bilges underneath the floorboards."

"OK. But what is it?"

"A piece of iron bar. There were a few on board – he uses them as weights in some of the smaller pots, it seems. But this one has blood and hair on it, and if I know anything, I'd say we will be able to match it to the wound on Terry Halpin's head."

"Ah, right. But I'm not sure that we'll need it now," Lyons said.

"Oh? How come?"

"Halpin is going for the temporarily insane plea, and I think they may buy it upstairs, so he'll probably be committed before he can stand trial. I think the Chief Super may go for it too. It's a lot simpler, especially with all this Maltese crap mixed in."

"Cripes! Right. What do you think about that?"

"Ah, it doesn't bother me too much. It will still go down as a home goal in the stats, and we got a couple of other bad guys off the streets while we were at it."

"Well, you know best about these things. I'll just file this away then in case we need it later on."

"Good idea."

Chapter Thirty-eight

Séan Mulholland eased his considerable bulk onto the high stool at the bar of McGlinchey's pub at the side of the Ballyconneely road.

"Ah, 'tis yourself, Séan. We don't see much of you out and about these days. Are ye keeping well?" the portly barman asked.

"I'm grand, Felim, grand."

"What can I get you? A pint is it?"

"No, not today, Felim. It's sort of official business I'm on. Just a cup of coffee – that would be lovely."

Felim turned his back on the sergeant to boil the kettle and prepare a cup of Nescafé, and presented it to Mulholland with a little jug of milk.

"I'm afraid we've no biscuits, Séan. What kind of official business is that then?"

"Ah, ye know. There's a story going round that some bloke from the North has been flogging smuggled spirits in these parts. I don't suppose you've come across him at all?"

"Oh, God no. Sure we wouldn't be into any of that sort of thing here. I could lose me license."

"That's what I thought, Felim. But sure you know, I have to make enquiries, as the saying goes."

"Of course, Séan. Have you found any of it anywhere hereabouts yet then?"

"Now that would be telling, Felim. But, no, not yet anyway."

Mulholland sat and drank his coffee, which was weak and not to his liking. But he persisted with it, and when he was done, he told Felim that he would be on his way.

"What do I owe you for the coffee, Felim."

"Ah, away with ye, for God's sake. It's just a drop of hot water."

Too right, Mulholland thought.

Then he said, "Do you know the kids' song about the ten green bottles hanging on the wall, Felim?"

"I do. Though I haven't heard it for years. Why?"

Mulholland nodded to the green bottle of Gordon's gin that he could see on the counter behind the bar.

"If I were you, I'd let that green bottle accidentally fall, Felim."

He turned and left the bar.

Epilogue

In the weeks that followed, Senan McGuire was charged with several counts of money laundering and other frauds. Surprisingly, he pleaded guilty to all of the charges. The detectives thought that he had probably been instructed to do so, in order that very few details of the various scams he was working would be revealed in open court. He was sentenced to eight years in jail, and much of his ill-gotten property was confiscated and sold by the Criminal Assets Bureau over the next two years.

Keith Gillespie had, true to his word, called on Pearse Street Garda station in Dublin and made a full statement. It wasn't needed in any case, but as soon as the ink was dry on the page, the lad vanished. No one knew what became of him, and he was never seen in Galway again.

There was much negotiation between Eoin Lawless, Detective Superintendent Mick Hays, and the DPP. Eventually Halpin pled guilty to the aiding and abetting, but claimed that the death of his son was down to self-defence. His psychological assessment determined that he was suffering from stress and was acting under duress. He was brought before the court, and was given a sentence of four years, all of which was suspended on condition that he sought treatment. He returned to his wife at Screebe.

Ardal McGuire – thanks to evidence provided by the Irish police – was also charged with money laundering. He didn't fare so well. He was attacked whilst on remand in Malta and died of an apparent heart attack in his cell one night when the door had mysteriously been left open. The Maltese police were not pursuing the matter and put the death down to natural causes.

Cónan O'Neill was charged with several crimes associated with the smuggling of alcohol, avoidance of excise duty and VAT and was given five years in prison. Lyons decided there was little to be served by pursuing Tadgh Deasy over his creative production of registration plates, but she had instructed Pascal Brosnan to keep a very close eye on his operation, and advise Lyons if there was anything at all untoward observed.

Séan Mulholland continued his tour of the small pubs all across his patch out west of Galway. It went much the same way in each of them, and by the time he'd finished, all of the publicans had mended their ways. None were prosecuted, and when Mulholland and Lyons were talking about the whole affair several months later, they agreed that the way he had chosen to handle it was best for all concerned.

Hays and Lyons completed the purchase of the property down by the river in Galway. It was divided into two flats, and each was let to junior members of the Garda at reasonable rates.

The much vaunted SOCU was finally given the green light in Galway. Lyons was, as expected, appointed head of the unit, and as a result, Eamon Flynn was made up to Senior Inspector to take control of the detectives.

List of Characters

Senior Detective Inspector Maureen Lyons – a feisty detective who is tougher than she seems, but always gets into a tight spot.

Detective Superintendent Mick Hays – in overall charge of the Galway Detective Unit. A seasoned policeman with loads of experience. As Maureen Lyons' life partner, he admires her occasionally unconventional techniques, but sometimes worries about her safety.

Detective Inspector Eamon Flynn – a tenacious member of the team who never lets up until he has his target well and truly cornered.

Detective Sergeant Sally Fahy – a pretty young officer with a keen instinct for identifying a wrongdoer.

Garda John O'Connor – a young Garda with a deep knowledge of all things technical. He just loves to get his hands on a computer, a mobile phone or anything technical that can lead to an arrest.

Sinéad Loughran – an incurably cheerful forensic officer with a rather barren love life.

Dr Julian Dodd – the sometimes sarcastic but highly skilled pathologist.

Sergeant Séan Mulholland – a wily old officer who runs Clifden Garda station in his own somewhat old-fashioned way. He's addicted to tea and chocolate biscuits.

Garda Pascal Brosnan – the Garda in charge of the small Garda station in Roundstone.

Garda Mary Fallon – lives in Clifden, but has been assigned to Roundstone where she assists Brosnan running the station.

Garda Peadar Tobin – a tall and handsome uniformed Garda from Clifden.

Chief Superintendent Finbarr Plunkett – a politically savvy senior officer who knows how to work the system to get what he needs for the team in Galway.

Inspector Poulis – a Maltese policeman who knows Mick Hays from a conference in Copenhagen.

Tadgh Deasy – a garageman with some very unorthodox sidelines.

Terry Halpin – a so-called builder who likes to travel, and get up to all sorts of mischief.

Keith Gillespie – Terry's mate who shares accommodation with him in a run-down flat in Galway city.

Senan McGuire – a Northern Ireland man in property development.

Ardal McGuire – Senan's brother who lives in Malta and runs an import-export company of sorts.

Cathal McDermott – a publican who finds it hard to make ends meet.

Cónan O'Neill – delivers bottles of liquor to pubs all over County Galway.

Elias Spiteri – a young man from Malta with a quick temper and an unfaithful girlfriend.

Hugh Halpin – Terry Halpin's father.

Delia – runs the bar at Kilnatrá with Cathal McDermott.

James McMahon – an architect from a prestigious practice in Galway city who is friendly with Mick Hays.

Teresa Doyle – Terry Halpin's girlfriend.

If you enjoyed this book, please let others know by leaving a quick review on Amazon. Also, if you spot anything untoward in the paperback, get in touch. We strive for the best quality and appreciate reader feedback.

editor@thebookfolks.com

www.thebookfolks.com

BOOKS BY DAVID PEARSON

In this series:

Murder on the Old Bog Road (Book 1)
Murder at the Old Cottage (Book 2)
Murder on the West Coast (Book 3)
Murder at the Pony Show (Book 4)
Murder on Pay Day (Book 5)
Murder in the Air (Book 6)
Murder at the Holiday Home (Book 7)
Murder on the Peninsula (Book 8)
Murder at the Races (Book 9)
Murder in a Safe Haven (Book 10)

In the Dublin Homicides Series:

A Deadly Dividend
A Fatal Liaison
The China Chapter
Lethal in Small Doses

A woman is found in a ditch, murdered. As the list of suspects grows, an Irish town's dirty secrets are exposed. Detective Inspector Mick Hays and DS Maureen Lyons are called in to investigate. But getting the locals to even speak to the police will take some doing. Will they find the killer in their midst?

When a nurse finds a reclusive old man dead in his armchair in his cottage, the local Garda surmise he was the victim of a burglary gone wrong. However, having suffered a violent death and there being no apparent robbery, Irish detectives are not so sure. It will take all their wits and training to track down the killer.

When the Irish police arrive at a road accident, they find evidence of a kidnapping and a murder. Detective Maureen Lyons is in charge of the case but, struggling with self-doubt, when a suspect slips through her fingers she must act fast to save her reputation and crack the case.

A man is found dead during the annual Connemara Pony Show. Panic spreads through the event when it is discovered he was murdered. Detective Maureen Lyons leads the investigation but the powers that be threaten to stonewall the inquiry.

Following a tip-off, Irish police lie in wait for a robbery. But the criminals cleverly evade their grasp. Meanwhile, a body is found beneath a cliff. DCI Mick Hays' chances of promotion will be blown unless he sorts out the mess.

After a wealthy businessman's plane crashes into bogland it is discovered the engine was tampered with. But who out of the three occupants was the intended target? DI Maureen Lyons leads the investigation, which points to shady dealings and an even darker crime.

A local businessman is questioned when a young woman is found dead in his property. His caginess makes him a prime suspect in what is now a murder inquiry. But with no clear motive and no evidence, detectives will have a hard task proving their case. They'll have to follow the money, even if it leads them into danger.

When a body is found on a remote Irish beach, detectives suspect foul play. Their investigation leads them to believe the death is connected to corruption in local government. But rather than have to hunt down the killer, he approaches them. With one idea in mind: revenge.

One of the highlights of Ireland's horseracing calendar is marred when a successful bookmaker is robbed and killed in the restrooms. DI Maureen Lyons investigates but is not banking on a troublemaker emerging from within the police ranks. Her team will have to deal with the shenanigans and catch a killer.

Printed in Great Britain
by Amazon

54696032R00135